Hallowed Hill

A Gothic Mystery

By Kit Campbell

TDP

For all who have suffered these past few years

Chapter One

September

AT THE TIME, Martie would have sworn they'd been driving through that forest for literally ever. They'd flown into Boston, rented a car, and barely survived the weird tunnels and ramps that existed just outside. But it hadn't been long before they'd been out of the city and into the trees. At first it had been nice—there weren't trees in Arizona, not really, and certainly not these huge ones that spread their canopies over the roads, creating a tunnel of leaves—but after a while, even trees can become commonplace. Perhaps even imposing. Creepy. Blocking out the sun and keeping the sky from you, draping the innards of the forest in shadow.

Or perhaps Martie had just been driving for too long.

Aunt Jessica, from the driver's side, turned up the radio and sang along, some '80s ballad that Martie had heard a gazillion times yet had somehow missed the words to. The trees clearly didn't bother Aunt Jessica, and probably the long drive didn't, either. She'd confided, halfway across the country, that this was the first time she'd gotten to go on a trip without any of her children in about eight years.

Aunt Jessica had five children. This was a major milestone, and she was living her best life.

Martie leaned against the glass, staring into the trees as they whizzed by. Too fast to really see anything. Why would anyone build a school out here, in the middle of the forest, away from everything and anyone?

Well, it said in the informational packet. Their "secure and scenic campus" was "located in such a way as to minimize distractions and inappropriate influences." But seriously.

"You excited?" Aunt Jessica asked for the thirteenth time.

Martie nodded without turning away from the window, not faulting her aunt for the repetition. Conversation was…hard. The events that had led them to be here, in the middle of the forest, Vermont, made Martie ache inside in a way she hated yet could not seem to fix. Even now, her eyes teared up. Martie wiped at them with the edge of her hoodie sleeve, trying not to be obvious.

Finally, the road, well-maintained even though there'd been no signs of civilization in ages, began to climb upward, slowly meandering across the face of what ended up being a fairly large hill. Aunt Jessica reached over, snapping the music off, as the sky became visible again and the trees retreated. The rental car crested and there, over the dashboard, it stood.

Greyson Preparatory Academy.

It looked like one would expect from the name. Most of the view was taken up by a large building, what had probably been a mansion of some sort early in its life, with two clear wings. The roof had a corner in the middle, like a barn, and a dozen gabled windows lined the top. The entire thing was painted white, except the roof and the very bottom of the building, both of which were a matte red. All the accents were black.

Martie frowned. It kind of looked like a massive dollhouse that someone had gone overboard on.

Instead of trees, the top of the hill was well-manicured. There was a lot of grass and many flowers, some even still blooming despite the fact that it was definitely heading into fall. The road switched from asphalt to cobblestone, of all things, so the remainder of the trip was unnecessarily bumpy.

Aunt Jessica pulled the car up in the curved driveway in front of the large building and parked. A woman was waiting for them, dressed in a black pantsuit, a leather portfolio in her hands.

"Okay, deep breaths," Aunt Jessica said, possibly talking to herself as much as Martie. "I hate to be that person, Martie, but I really, really want this to work out for you. Do your best, sweetie. But, you know, get the lay of the land before you get too crazy."

Martie forced a smile. Aunt Jessica didn't have to worry—she wanted to succeed here too. She didn't really know how, or why, this opportunity had fallen into her lap, but she wasn't going to look a gift horse in the mouth. Which, why, really, aren't you supposed to? Do horses bite? Do they hide spiders in there? Someone probably knew.

Martie took a deep breath before she pushed the car door open and slid out.

The woman—short, Latina—made her way down the front stairs, a practiced smile gracing her face. Her suit was tailored impeccably. Martie felt out of place in jeans and a hoodie. Aunt Jessica had gone all out—dark jeans, black ankle boots, a black blazer—but where she'd looked amazing that morning, she now looked shabby, compared to this other woman.

"Martina Torsney, yes?" The woman looked down at her portfolio for a moment before meeting Martie's eyes. "We're so pleased to have you joining us. How was the drive?"

Long. Full of trees. Oh, so many trees. "Fine."

"And this must be your legal guardian?" Her eyes moved to Aunt Jessica, sweeping over her. Probably judging her store-bought, untailored, slightly out-of-date clothes.

"Yes, this is my aunt, Jessica Williamson."

"We were so sorry to hear about your parents, of course. How are you doing?"

God, the number of times Martie had heard that statement. "I'm sorry, you are?"

The woman blinked. "Goodness, didn't I say? I'm so sorry. I'm Susana Molina, Head of Admissions here at Greyson. It's almost time for dinner, but you should have time to settle in a bit before, or we could send your meal to your room, if you're tired. Will you be staying to help Martina get settled?"

This last bit was directed at Aunt Jessica. Martie glanced at her—she'd gone around the back of the car and was unloading the bags. Martie hadn't brought a lot, and it was thrown in whatever bags they'd salvaged from Martie's parents. Not the sort of lot Ms. Molina probably saw much, if ever, here.

Aunt Jessica looked over at Martie, her question obvious in her gaze. Swallowing, Martie glanced around the campus again. It was something out of a movie, nothing out of place. Besides the large central building, there were two other buildings visible, identical square ones on each end of a wing, with matching architecture and colors. There were a few students about, though not close. Martie was wildly out of place, and in that moment, she wanted nothing more than to climb back into the car and go back to Arizona, even if it meant spending the rest of her high school career sharing a room with Aunt Jessica's oldest daughter—who was seven—and surviving the chaos of that house, with its echoes of what she had lost.

No. She had to do this. It was a clean slate, a way to move past what had happened in the past few months. There would be nothing to remind her here, and she needed to be able to provide for herself. Aunt Jessica wouldn't need to add Martie onto her list of worries anymore.

Martie shook her head as little as she could.

Aunt Jessica placed the last bag on the ground and brushed her hands together. "I should be going," she said. "I've got a long way to go tonight." She hugged Martie tight. "Call me if you need anything," she whispered in her ear. "You're going to do great. I love you!"

She climbed back into the car, waving as she drove back down the road. All too soon, the car had disappeared over the crest of the hill, where the canopies of the trees waited.

There weren't any trees up here on the top of the hill, actually. Maybe they felt like they marred the view. Or maybe they felt like there were already enough trees.

Kind of a weird hill, to be fair. It was more of a mesa, or maybe it'd been flattened on the top. Or maybe Martie didn't know anything about New England geology.

"Right," said Ms. Molina, clapping her hands together. "Go ahead and leave your bags. I'll have them sent to your room." Tucking her portfolio under one arm, she headed to the left, her heels clicking on the cobblestones. How could she walk like that? Martie would be afraid of losing a heel to the mortar. "You'll have read the informational packet, I assume."

"Yes."

She nodded, as if nothing else could have been expected. "You'll start classes tomorrow. We're a few weeks into the school year, but you should have no problems catching back up. Everything you'll need for tonight is in your dorm building—showers, dinner, et cetera."

She droned on, but Martie let her attention wander, making sure the sleeves of her hoodie were pulled all the way over her palms. After all, the informational packet had been very thorough. A map of the campus, quiet hours, a list of amenities. Certainly way nicer than any other school Martie had ever gone to. That was part of the point. She'd seen pictures too, having stalked the place obsessively when the acceptance letter had first arrived. Of course, she'd also never heard of the place before the acceptance letter. It could have all been some sort of cruel joke.

But it was different, seeing it in person. The pictures had mostly been in the spring, when the flowers were in full bloom, or in the winter so you could see how elegant the buildings looked amid the snow. And they'd all been during the day. They were definitely getting into dusk now, the sky streaked with orange.

Some weird stones right near the edge of the hill caught Martie's eye. They didn't match the carefully laid out grounds, instead listing at weird angles in places. They were kind of in a grid, kind of like...

...like a graveyard. And God knew she'd been in enough of those, lately.

Ms. Molina laid a hand on her shoulder. Martie jumped. Ms. Molina smiled again, more sincere this time, but Martie saw in her look what everyone gave her these days.

Pity.

"It's the old family graveyard," Ms. Molina supplied. "A lot of families buried their dead on their own land, especially when they weren't close to a town or other population center. When the Greysons left the property to the school, one of the obligations the school agreed to was to leave the graveyard in peace."

Martie appreciated not being asked if she was okay again. "Did the family live here long?"

"No. Just a decade or so."

Martie glanced back at the graveyard. She easily counted eight gravestones and suspected there might be more in the light of day, or perhaps out of sight down the side of the hill. Eight people in ten years seemed like a lot, but, hey, those were different times. Most of them were probably children.

Interesting, though, that they were just plain gravestones. No big, old mausoleums or creepy crying angel statues. "I would have thought that they would have...put more money into the family graveyard."

"Maybe they meant to, once they got established."

Ms. Molina squeezed Martie's shoulder once, and they continued on their way.

She led the way toward the dorm building. Once they'd gotten far enough from the main building, Martie could see that there were two additional buildings behind it, which, from the map she'd received, she knew to be the teachers' quarters and the recreation center. Most teachers lived on campus, since they were in the middle of a sea of trees. There was a village somewhere nearby-ish, half an hour maybe, but Martie wouldn't want to drive home, in the dark, through all those trees, either. Things lived in them. Like bears, maybe. Or moose. Or sasquatch, for all she knew.

There was a library in the main building, according to the amenity list. She should get a book about Vermont. And maybe horses.

As they reached the door, Ms. Molina waved her ID in front of a pad, which clicked and turned green. "This way," she said as she pulled the door open. They stepped into an honest-to-god foyer, complete with atrium. An ornately-carved staircase curved up to the second floor, and a walkway wove along the atrium on both that and the third floor. The walls were wood-paneled and gleamed. Good lord, it was someone's job to polish the things. Above, a large skylight let in the gathering dark, and plants were strategically placed around the edges of the room.

"Bit sparse, I know." Ms. Molina pursed her lips. "But the idea is to not be too distracting. This is a functional building, after all."

A bit sparse? This looked like the sort of old, elegant building you'd see in a movie. But what did Martie know?

The stairs creaked as they headed up to the second floor, as did the floor as they wandered along the corridor toward a less showy staircase heading to the third. And the staircase to the third floor. And the third floor itself.

"These buildings date to about 1890," Ms. Molina said, reading Martie's mind. "Ah, here we are." They'd stopped at the second room down the corridor. There was a brass plate to the right side, which said "302," and, below that, an engraved plate that had Martie's name and another on it. "Hayden will be your roommate. This is her second year with us, so she'll be able to answer any questions you might have."

"Sure," Martie said.

Ms. Molina knocked twice. There was no answer from inside, so after a moment, she fished a key card out of her pocket and waved it by a panel just above the doorknob. The door clicked open almost immediately. Martie peered around Ms. Molina as she pushed the door open. It was smaller than Martie had imagined it would be. Both beds inside were lofted, with desks and dressers underneath, and there were two doors across from each other that must be closets. Aside from that, though, there was maybe enough floor space between the beds for four people to sit in a circle, and there was no window, though there was a skylight overhead.

"Here." Ms. Molina dropped a card into Martie's hand. It had her face and name on it and was attached to a lanyard, so she could wear it around her neck. "You'll use this to access your room, this building, the rec center, and the main building. It's also tied to your account, should you need to purchase anything. As a scholarship student, you'll have a monthly allowance, as was discussed in your acceptance letter. Do you need us to order anything for you? A winter coat perhaps?"

"Just to double check—my allowance is $500 a month?"

"Yes, that's correct. If you need more for something specific, there is a process to request additional funds."

Additional funds? This place was insane. Five hundred dollars a month was insane. That note in the acceptance letter had been just one of many things that had seemed like a red flag. Too good to be true. That some fancy-ass top-ranked boarding school out East had decided to offer Martie a scholarship for the remainder of high school, one that she'd never heard of, and that they were going to give her $500 for books, supplies, and whatever the hell else she wanted? Yeah, right. Discreetly, Martie pinched herself, just in case. Being here, standing in this room—which, to be fair, was a perfectly normal-looking dorm—was surreal. It still felt like the whole thing could dissipate into smoke, that she'd wake up any moment and be home, in her own bed, in her own house, with her parents—

No. Not going there. "I would appreciate a list of clothing items you'd recommend for the winter,"

Martie said. Adults liked it when you pretended you were on top of things. "As well as anything else that might help me with my studies here."

Ms. Molina did look pleased. Score. "Of course. I'll email it to you. Now, this is your side here." She indicated the left side of the room. "Your bags will be brought up shortly. We've taken the liberty of procuring you a laptop which should be sufficient for your schoolwork." Said laptop was sitting on the desk, shiny and brand new. Martie pinched herself again.

Everything stayed put.

"I know the rooms aren't much to look at." Ms. Molina put her hands on her hips, surveying the room herself. "That's on purpose. Most of our students come from households where they've wanted for nothing. It is our intention to give people a more...realistic view of how the world works."

Admirable. And, hey, it was only one other person. And that person wasn't a seven-year-old.

Of course, that person was probably a stuck-up rich kid, so trade-offs, Martie guessed.

From behind them, a knock sounded on the door frame. Martie turned to find a girl her same age there—and alas, she looked like every stuck-up rich kid in every movie Martie had ever seen. Her long, silky blonde hair was pulled back into a high ponytail, and she wore a cardigan with the school's emblem over a white blouse.

"Good evening, Hayden," Ms. Molina supplied.

"Oh, goodness, is this her?" Martie tensed. Of course her roommate, no doubt used to the other rich kids who went to this school, would be disappointed in Martie. But without waiting for an answer, Hayden threw her arms around Martie. "I'm so happy to meet you! We're going to be such good friends! I've been waiting for*ever,* and I was so excited when Ms. Molina said you'd be here today!"

Martie hugged her back awkwardly. This was some sort of act, right? Something to show Ms. Molina how mature Hayden was being about the less-than-ideal assignment of roommate. No doubt as soon as they were alone, it would be a different story.

Ms. Molina smiled again. "I'll email you that list." Then she stepped out into the hallway, closing the door behind her.

Hayden peeled herself off of Martie. Okay, here it came.

"God, I'm sorry." Hayden climbed up onto her bed and hung her legs over the edge, blinking down at Martie. "Everyone says I'm too clingy. I didn't make you uncomfortable, did I?"

Huh, no change in personality yet. Hesitantly, Martie copied Hayden. The bed was soft—much softer than one would expect from a lofted bed. She let herself sink into it, staring across at Hayden. "Am I your first roommate for the year?"

"Yep!" Hayden swung her legs. "Normally you keep the same roommate the whole time, but my one for last year didn't come back."

"Oh? Why not?"

Hayden shrugged. "No idea. But tell me about yourself! All I know is your name."

Great, just like being a new student anywhere. And it sounded like Hayden hadn't been told that Martie was here on scholarship, so trying things out on Hayden might be a good way to streamline things before being confronted with the student body at large. "Well, I'm from Arizona. Near Tucson."

"Oh, how exciting!" Hayden rested her head in her hands and her elbows on her knees. "We went to Flagstaff once, for skiing." She cocked her head to one side, then hesitantly added, "Aren't there reservations down there?"

"What does that have to do with anything?"

Hayden went bright pink. "Never mind."

Martie was used to that. She had dark hair and dark eyes, and a complexion just tan enough that it bothered people that liked to categorize other people. People had offered a dozen or so different ethnicities over the years, and Martie tried to approach each of them with the same level of confusion. People usually backed off after that. It didn't help that she had a noticeable smattering of freckles across her nose, which sometimes made people more determined to figure out "what" she was.

Weird thing was, she didn't know. Her parents had cut ties with their families before she was born—something about her parents not marrying the "right type"—so Martie had no idea what her ethnic background was. She didn't think they celebrated anything that pointed to anything in particular, and her parents were—had been—the same ambiguous shade that she was. Aunt Jessica was the only extended family member that Martie knew, and while she was lighter than Martie's mother had been, it still didn't really mean anything.

"Anyway," Martie said, "I go by Martie, I'm sixteen, and I'm a sophomore."

"What school did you go to down there?" Hayden asked, seemingly grateful for the change in topic.

"Just my local neighborhood high school."

"Oh." Hayden crinkled her nose. "And then your parents decided to send you here, to get a better education?"

A pang echoed in Martie's heart. No. She had to be strong. Focus on the rest of the statement. "Actually, it was kind of weird. I got an acceptance letter and a scholarship in the mail without ever applying to the school."

"Really?" Hayden widened her eyes. "Wow, scholarships are super rare. I think they only do one at a time, and not all the time. Someone must have put you in for it. Not your parents, though? I guess not; they would have told you."

Hayden obviously meant well. It wouldn't hurt to tell her, would it? Martie hesitated. No, she should be honest. There was no way she was going to fit in here no matter what, and pretending that she was just another rich kid whose parents had paid her way was just going to lead to trouble in the future. She'd seen enough teen movies to know that the lies always came out eventually, usually in the worst way possible. She'd get along by being herself, or at least try to. "My parents are dead."

"Oh, God, I'm so sorry." Hayden covered her mouth with her hands. "I keep sticking my foot in my mouth. I mean, I always have, but I've, I've been practicing. I wanted to make a good impression. I am so, so sorry."

Martie got an image of Hayden standing in front of a mirror, practicing introducing herself to Martie. Hayden was going to be okay. "Hey, let's go get some food. There's a cafeteria in here, right?"

"Yes!" Hayden swung down off the edge of the bed, ponytail following, then grimaced. "Crap, I forgot that the people underneath us can hear when I do that. I mean, uh, dang."

A smile crept onto Martie's face. It felt good. Maybe this was the new start she'd hoped it would be.

Hayden led the way out into the hallway. "The cafeteria's in the basement. It's kind of awful, but the food is decent."

As Martie followed her out, the overhead lights flickered and dimmed, releasing a low hum at the same time. Hayden trailed off, staring up at them, then laughed nervously. "Old buildings, you know?"

But as they made their way down the hallway, each light did the same thing as they passed underneath.

Chapter Two

MARTIE BLINKED awake, holding a hand between her eyes and the bright light shining down from overhead. It took a moment before she remembered where she was, but then it all came flooding back—staying with Aunt Jessica, the surprise acceptance, the flight, the trees. Across the room, Hayden had her pillow over her head, no doubt to block the sun filtering in through the skylight.

As quietly as she could manage, Martie climbed out of her bed, heading to her closet. After dinner, she'd returned to find her bags had arrived. She'd put out a few belongings on her desk and her clothes into her dresser, and had discovered that her closet was full of school clothing—slacks and pleated skirts and button-down shirts and polos, sweaters and cardigans, even some nicer shoes. The sweaters, cardigans, and polos had the Greyson Preparatory Academy emblem on them, and they were mostly dark gray or navy.

This whole situation still felt oddly like a dream. Her grades had been good back home, but not exemplary. Nothing that would warrant receiving a scholarship to some place like this. In her research, Martie had learned that the school only had sixty students at a time—fifteen for each grade—and that graduates typically went on to great things. They also had a huge waiting list, which made her own acceptance that much weirder.

She couldn't help but feel that a mistake had been made, and that sooner or later, someone would figure that out, and then she'd be back where she was before.

Martie pulled out a skirt, sweater, and blouse and laid them nicely on the edge of her bed, then wandered out into the hallway. The sole restroom was farther along the corridor, then down a side hallway, all the way at the end, since apparently whoever built these buildings didn't believe the dorm rooms should have windows. It was divided into two sections—the first part, when you entered, had three showers in it, and then the toilets and sinks were farther in, in a move that must have made sense to someone at some point. Martie had both rooms to herself.

She did what she needed to, then went to wash her hands in the sink. The water was frigid. Martie finished rinsing the soap off, shaking her hands a few times.

When she looked up into the mirror, there was a girl standing behind her, close enough to touch her shoulder.

Martie whirled around, but the bathroom was empty behind her.

Tentatively, Martie turned back to the mirror. No one. No sign of anyone.

Okay, weird. Someone playing a trick, maybe. Martie dried her hands with the air dryer and headed back through the shower room, but nothing had changed. She peeked behind each shower curtain—all already partially open—but there was no one, and nowhere else to hide.

Well, maybe they'd run all the way out again. Martie shrugged and headed back to her room.

The clothes she'd laid out were everywhere. Skirt on the back of the desk chair, sweater in the middle of the floor, blouse hanging by one sleeve off the back of the bed. She definitely hadn't left them like that. So last night had been too good to be true. Figured. "What the hell, Hayden?"

Hayden groggily raised her head from under her pillow. "What?"

Martie hesitated. "Have you been up yet?"

Hayden rolled over, rubbing at one eye. "No, why?" She blinked a few times. "Why'd you throw your clothes all over?"

She had to be pretending, right? Surely Hayden had gotten up, flung Martie's clothes about, and then had crawled back into her bed to pretend to be asleep. But the confusion on her face—it seemed real.

"I didn't," Martie said.

Hayden blinked again. "What?"

But if it hadn't been Hayden... Martie stared at her clothes, then bent over to grab her sweater. It was noticeably cold, as if it'd been left outside. "No one can come into our room, right?" Maybe the skylight could open, and a breeze had come in? But no, one look told Martie that the skylight was sealed, and what sense did that make, anyway? "Weird."

Hayden sat up, frowning. "It's an old building."

She'd said that last night, when the lights had flickered. But what did the building being old have to do with her clothes?

Mystery unsolved, Martie got dressed while Hayden ran to the bathroom, finding a pair of white tights—the nice, thick kind—in her dresser. Okay, deep breaths. First day in a new school. First day in a weird, super fancy, rich-kid school. She just needed to get the lay of the land, like Aunt Jessica had said, without drawing too much attention to herself.

"Right," Hayden said as they headed down to breakfast. This morning, she'd wrapped her long, blonde hair into the sleekest French twist Martie had ever seen. "Ms. Molina will come get you and get you your schedule. All the classes are in the main building, unless you've got a physical education one. Actually, if you don't, you might be assigned an extracurricular there. Supposed to get regular exercise and all that." She smoothed her own skirt. "'A Greyson Academy student must treat their body like they treat their mind,'" she said formally, like she was quoting something.

"Great," Martie said. What kind of weird athletics did they offer here? Martie had done taekwondo on and off back home, when they could afford it, but it was hard to imagine that sort of thing appealing to the kids here. Maybe…golf? Or whatever that sport on horseback with the clubs was. Neither of those seemed to need a rec center, but whatever.

The lights flickered again as they descended the final, back staircase into the basement. Bits of conversation floated upward, and Martie slowed. When she and Hayden had gone to eat the night before, they must have been off, schedule-wise, because they'd hardly seen anyone else. Now it sounded like the whole building was present.

This was fine. Really. Had to happen sometime. Sure, having eaten something first would have been ideal, but it was what it was. Martie descended the final few stairs and stepped into chaos. There were girls everywhere, eating and laughing and talking in groups. She tried to stay with Hayden as the other girl moved through the noise toward the food line, wishing people good morning exuberantly and mostly getting more reticent replies back. But people lapsed into silence when they noticed Martie, watching her path through the room.

Martie swallowed. *This is fine. I'm fine.* If she'd gotten through the last few months intact, she could survive breakfast.

"So, this is her?" Martie turned to find another girl, similar to her own coloring, though her hair was pulled back into an immaculate bun, standing behind her, arms crossed over her chest. "The special scholarship student?"

Great, how did this girl know that? As far as Martie knew, Hayden hadn't had a chance to talk to anyone after last night, and if Hayden hadn't known, it seemed like no one should. "Uh, hi. I'm Martie."

The other girl did not introduce herself. "I'm watching you, Scholarship. If you think you can waltz in here and just take what other people have earned, you are going to be sorely disappointed." She sniffed loudly. "None of the other scholarship students have lasted. No doubt you won't, either." Turning on her heel, she sauntered off across the room, joining a group near the door, which immediately descended into whispers.

That hadn't gone great. Martie forced herself to turn away and back toward the food. Hayden was waiting, her cheeks pink again.

"Don't worry about Sinclair," she murmured. "She doesn't like anybody, especially not anybody who she feels might be challenging her."

"Am I?" Martie asked. "Challenging her, I mean."

Hayden shrugged. "You've got to be pretty smart, right? Since you earned a scholarship and all, and without even applying for it yourself. Sinclair's normally ranked at the top of our grade, so, yeah, she does probably think you are."

Hayden headed toward the food again. Martie followed, keeping her head up high, to show that Sinclair hadn't gotten to her. But that weird feeling again, the one that said she shouldn't be here, that this was too good to be true, twisted through her insides. Why had she gotten a scholarship? Why her? There had to be tons of other kids around the country who had better grades, better extracurriculars, better everything. She was just a pretty good student from a small town in the bottom of Arizona. She'd never done anything noteworthy in her life.

"What did she mean?" she asked Hayden as they retrieved their trays. Food here operated in a way Martie was used to—get a tray, go down the line and ask for what you wanted—but was a much higher quality than she'd seen before. There were waffles and bacon, eggs— five different kinds—and French toast, eggs benedict and something that looked vaguely like curry. "About the other scholarship students, I mean."

"I'm not sure." Hayden gave her a small smile. "We don't get many, like I told you. I haven't known any before."

The rest of breakfast passed quickly enough. Hayden invited Martie to sit with a few of the other girls—two more from their grade, and a couple who were freshmen—who were friendly enough and didn't seem to share Sinclair's sentiments. Martie could feel Sinclair watching her, or maybe it was one of the other girls she was sitting with, because she could feel eyes on her. But she didn't turn to give them the satisfaction.

Ms. Molina collected her in the atrium after breakfast and led her to the main building while everyone else hurried to class. The graveyard was more noticeable in the morning light, and there definitely were more gravestones than she'd originally seen. Weird that the school hadn't landscaped around it to hide it. That wouldn't technically be disturbing the graveyard, after all.

It was creepy, knowing there were dead bodies a short distance from where she was sleeping.

Well, depending on how long they'd been dead, maybe they weren't there anymore. But still.

"Here's your schedule." Ms. Molina handed her a matching leather portfolio to her own, the Greyson Academy emblem embossed on the front. "Go ahead and open it."

Inside, there was a pad of paper, a fancy pen, and a pocket with several sheets in it. The first was her schedule. The second was a list of the sophomores, complete with pictures. Everyone looked very professional in them, in their uniforms. Fifteen, as expected, eight girls and seven boys. Well, seven girls and seven boys. Martie was not among them.

"Ms. Molina, do you know who submitted my name for the scholarship?"

"I don't, I'm sorry. It was anonymous."

"Is that normal?"

Ms. Molina frowned. "Well, it's hard to say. We so rarely have scholarship positions open up. But whoever it was included enough information that we didn't need to contact them again, and anything else we needed we could get from your previous school."

Martie fidgeted with the edge of the picture of her classmates. There was an empty circle in the bottom row that simply said "Future Student" underneath it. "Can you tell me more about the scholarship process in general? Like, when it's determined a spot should be opened, and what the selection criteria is?"

"You're going to be late for your first period, Martina." Ms. Molina tucked her own portfolio under her arm. "Don't worry about it, okay? No matter what the process was, you made it in, and we will treat you just as well as we treat the rest of our students. You have nothing to worry about. Now, would you like me to walk you to your first class?"

Martie's first class was history, on the first floor of the main building. Unlike its imposing exterior, the interior had been modified to resemble a normal school. Though the floors were tile and not just linoleum, and the fluorescent lights lining the ceiling were a more calming, natural color than she'd seen before, it was noticeably a school. Lockers lined the wall in a formal charcoal gray, made of wood instead of metal. All the lockers were in this one section, since there were so few students overall. Less than it seemed like the school would hold, but perhaps the idea was to make sure everyone had enough space. The only part of the school that still held the ornate interior from when it must have been a mansion was the main entrance and the offices immediately next door.

On the back of Martie's schedule was a map. She studied it, following Ms. Molina by the sound of her heels on the floor. Rather than by grade, classes were grouped by subject. All history classrooms together, all science, all math. Made sense, since teachers could coordinate with each other and share resources. Come to think of it, her own school had been somewhat similar, especially for science and math. The rest of the classes had been a little less organized.

However, there were only a handful of teachers for each subject, and all the classes were in the west wing, the one closest to her dorm. The east wing was just a black box on the map, which was labeled "Other." Nowhere was the library she'd read about mentioned.

Ms. Molina's heels paused, and she knocked on one of the doors. A muffled reply came from inside. Martie frowned, unable to make it out, though it sounded angry, but Ms. Molina pulled the door open anyway. "I'm dropping off Martina Torsney," she announced to the room, then stepped aside so Martie could enter.

Martie slowly stepped inside. Instead of desks, all fourteen other sophomores sat around a long, oval table in the middle of the room, and all of them were staring at her. The teacher, an older, round woman, stood at the far end of the room next to a whiteboard. She, too, stared, her face pulled into a massive frown.

Behind Martie, Ms. Molina released the door. Her heels echoed down the hallway.

Martie tightened her grip on her portfolio. "Good morning," she said, trying to get on top of the situation. "I'm Martina, but you can call me Martie."

"Lovely," drawled the teacher in a strong Texan accent. "But you are disrupting class, Miss Torsney. Please take your seat so we can continue."

Oof. Martie quickly crossed the room and sank into the only available seat, in between a tall, dark-skinned boy and a girl in a hijab. Neither of them paid her any mind as they transferred their attention back to the teacher and the white board. Martie discreetly pulled her schedule out of her portfolio. Mrs. Weissman. Comparative history? Comparing it to what?

"Who can give me another example?" Mrs. Weissman said. Two maps were projected onto the white board behind her, one of the Mediterranean, and one of eastern Asia. No words were projected or written to add any clarification.

Across the table, Sinclair raised her hand. "Reliance on Western sources has received criticism from Chinese historians in the past." She smirked at Martie.

Martie forced herself to nod, like she had any idea what was going on. She flipped through the sheets in her portfolio, on the off chance that someone had summarized her classes for her. But no, it was all administrative.

The boy next to her was now arguing with Sinclair, something about how exterior sources of the proper time period could still be a valuable resource when examining history. If only someone would say something that would ground Martie, give her an idea of what the heck they were discussing. A time period, a name, a place.

Aside from her portfolio, she also had a shoulder bag. Martie had gone through it that morning to get a feel of what was in there. It was mostly pencils and pens and notebooks, normal school supplies. She didn't remember there being any loose papers in there, but it wouldn't hurt to look.

Hayden tentatively raised her hand. "But couldn't we, you know, translate Chinese sources of the time period and add those into the discussion?"

"That does run the risk of only adding in propaganda," another boy, sandy-haired, replied.

"Hence the use of outside sources!" concluded the boy next to Martie excitedly.

"Outside sources are also biased." Sinclair sniffed.

There were no loose papers, no folders. Martie fished out a notebook and flipped through it. It was a little crazy to think that someone might have made a copy of the notes for the year in them, but so was $500 a month to do whatever with. But, alas, no, all the notebooks were empty.

There was no help for it. Martie raised her hand.

Mrs. Weissman zeroed in on her immediately. "Yes, Miss Torsney?"

"I'm sorry, but what are we talking about?"

Everyone else at the table turned to look at her. Martie wanted to melt into the floor, but, come on, it was unreasonable to expect her to know what she'd missed for the first month of school without any sort of notes. Back home, in Arizona, they'd kind of blown through Ancient Egypt and Greece and Rome and had been moving into the Middle Ages when Martie left.

"We are comparing the formation and governance of the Roman Empire to the Han Dynasty," Mrs. Weissman answered in short, clipped tones.

No, they were arguing about the legitimacy of source material, but at least this explained the maps on the board. "Thank you."

Mrs. Weissman nodded once and seemed to take Martie's interruption as a cue to move the discussion back into lecturing. Martie pulled out a notebook to take notes in, but noticed that about half of the table had nothing. Sinclair just sat with her hands folded on the table, smirking at anyone who was doing more than just listening. Was she even listening? Maybe not. She'd probably memorized the entire subject just so she could be superior about everything.

Martie wasn't competing against Sinclair. She had to remember that, despite the urge to shove something in Sinclair's face. In the movies and whatnot that had portrayed scholarships, there was always some sort of terms to the scholarship. Some level of grades to keep up. But Ms. Molina had implied that because Martie was in, she was in. So, in theory, she didn't need to be top of the class or anything like that.

Still, it would probably be good to ask. Next time she saw Ms. Molina. The last thing she needed was to be kicked out suddenly because she'd violated some rule she wasn't aware of.

This classroom was a little strange. Unlike the hallway, it looked more like a boardroom than a school. The wood paneling had been left in place, and a rich, ornamental carpet covered the floor. The table itself was real wood of some sort, cherry maybe, thick and sturdy. And all the chairs were ergonomic and cushioned. Martie could sit here for hours before her butt started to hurt.

Soon, though, class must have been over, because everyone stood and started packing up anything they'd gotten out. No bell, though, or other auditory signal. Martie followed suit, trying to figure out what the sign had been. The only clock in the classroom was behind the table.

Once she'd gotten her stuff together, Martie approached Mrs. Weissman. The teacher had settled behind a heavy oak desk in the corner and was typing on her computer. "Mrs. Weissman?"

"Vicemen."

"What?"

"It's pronounced Viceman," Mrs. Weissman said, suddenly dropping into a German accent. Maybe the Texan accent was to cover that.

"Oh, sorry, Mrs. Weissman." Martie used the correct pronunciation this time. "I was wondering if there was a way I could get a study guide or some other resource so I could catch up to where the rest of the class is." She flashed her best student smile, one that normally showed her teachers that she was a good student who was trying her best.

"Study guide?" Mrs. Weissman echoed, Texan accent back in place. "There is no study guide for this class."

"Oh, then—"

"I do not know how they did things in your last school, Miss Torsney, but here at Greyson, we expect students to think for themselves." She glowered at Martie. "I give you the subject at hand, and you go and find out information about it. This also teaches you to vet your resources and form your own opinions, instead of those you are handfed. Now, I have given you our current topic of conversation, and you have heard the input of your classmates. It is up to you to supplement that."

What? Martie blinked twice, but Mrs. Weissman's face hadn't changed. "Do you have any recommendations?" she tried.

"You have access to several academic journal databases through the school's system." Mrs. Weissman transferred her attention back to her screen. "Good day, Miss Torsney."

"Good day, Mrs. Weissman," Martie echoed automatically.

Good Lord, what kind of school was this? What made it worse was that Martie could see the argument behind it. But she'd always been good at memorizing things and figuring out what her teachers wanted. What if she was no good at how this school worked? Even if there were no terms on her scholarship, surely the school would get rid of kids who were falling behind. Maybe that was what had happened to Hayden's last roommate.

No, she had to be more optimistic. She could figure this out, given a little time. She had to be successful here, or she'd be letting—

Be letting—

She took a deep breath. She'd be letting her parents down.

She had to be able to think about them. It would be cruel to erase their memory, like they had never been. She loved them too much to do that. But that strange anxiety that always came now, when she thought of them, swirled around her heart. She straightened the sleeves of her cardigan, making sure they were all the way down to her wrists.

Hayden was waiting for her out in the hall. "Intense, right? You holding up okay?"

"I'll figure it out."

"Can I see your schedule?"

Martie handed it over, realizing she hadn't really looked at it too closely herself. Bit weird, wasn't it, that she'd had no input on it? Though she supposed they'd mostly put her into classes based on what she'd been in at her last school. Still, there had to be electives, right? Sports?

"Pretty good," Hayden said, handing the schedule back. "I'm in your math class next. I much prefer math, don't you? No having to prove that you have research to back up your statements or being graded on whether or not you can sway other people to your point of view."

"Is that a thing we have to do?"

"Sometimes." Hayden sighed, pushing her hair behind her shoulders. "I know it's good for me, but the numbers are what they are, and there's no argument about that. It's nice to have something be concretely right or wrong."

That sick feeling settled back into Martie's stomach.

Math was up a floor. Martie thought they might have to backtrack to the lobby and use the grand staircase, but Hayden led her to a secondary staircase in the middle of the hallway. It was very narrow; Martie couldn't walk beside Hayden.

"This was a servant's staircase, I think." Hayden's voice echoed weirdly. It wasn't concrete, not like the staircases had been back home, but the stairs were worn wood, and there were no windows or decoration on the walls. "Supposed to be able to easily get between floors without having to share a staircase with the family."

The staircase had a landing at the second floor, then continued on upward. A large wooden door stood propped open on the landing.

"It's just through here," Hayden supplied as her foot reached the landing.

Almost in slow motion, the doorstop holding the door open slid out of place, and the door slammed shut.

Hayden squeaked and jumped backward, knocking into Martie. "Crap, that almost got me. Sorry." Laughing awkwardly, she climbed back onto the landing and twisted the door handle.

It didn't turn. It was locked.

"Weird." Hayden tried a couple more times, but the handle just clicked uselessly. "This hasn't ever happened before. Normally they don't lock the doors during the day." She pulled a couple of times, but despite its obvious age, it was a solid door, and it didn't budge. "I must have bounced the landing too hard."

That didn't seem likely. Hayden was 110 pounds, maybe, and the landing was constructed as well as the rest of the building. But, still, what was the alternative?

"We'd better go back down." Hayden sighed. "We're going to be late."

Martie turned and started hurrying back down the stairs. "Speaking of which, how do you know when the period is—"

A loud click came from behind them. Martie turned. It was hard to see around Hayden, but the door at the top of the stairs was open again, doorstop back in place.

"Oh!" Hayden changed course. "Someone must have heard us and opened it."

Martie followed Hayden up and out onto the second floor. There was no one in sight, aside from a couple of kids a couple of classrooms down.

"This way!" Hayden headed to the right. Martie glanced around once more, then followed.

The math classroom was set up more like a standard classroom, with about twenty desks in rows. Still nicer than your standard high school desk, actually wood, and the chair was separate instead of being connected. There was carpet in here too, though it was a single gray color, and the windows, three of them, had full curtains, valences and everything, in a rich maroon color.

"Nice of you to find your way," Sinclair drawled from the front row. "I was beginning to think we'd need to send out a search party. You know, if the layout is too complicated, you're welcome to go back to your single-story cinderblock building out in the deserts."

You'd think a school of this caliber would be anti-bullying, but maybe that wouldn't allow people to think for themselves. Or maybe they thought you had to be ruthless to be successful.

"Hey, Sinclair," she heard herself say and tried to lock down on the impulse, but it was too late. "What are you named after, the gas station or the guy who wrote *The Jungle*?"

The room, which had been brimming with quiet chatter, went still. Beside her, Hayden put her hands over her mouth.

Sinclair went an impressive shade of purple for a moment before visibly pulling herself back together. "It's a Scottish clan, named for Saint-Clair-sur-Elle." She said the name in a perfect French accent. "But I wouldn't expect you to know that."

Martie shrugged. "I thought maybe your parents owned the gas station chain. You never know."

Sinclair opened her mouth, but their teacher swept in. "Martina, right?" he said. "You can sit wherever. We'll be going over basic trigonometry principles today." He handed her a packet of paper and then swept his hand out to indicate she should sit.

Martie took an empty seat in the second row, next to Hayden and one of the windows. The packet was a study guide, going over what they'd covered so far this year, if the dates on each page were anything to go by.

Didn't believe in study guides here at Greyson, her ass.

This, at least, she knew. Or had started. Maybe she wouldn't fail out after all.

The view out the window was pretty great, she had to admit. Martie could just see the edge of the lawn and cobblestone drive—but not the graveyard, luckily—and then the sea of trees beyond. They were starting to change into their autumn splendor, something she'd heard about but had never really experienced. Yes, they had trees in Arizona, but not that many, and they were far enough south that the whole season thing got a little confused.

Something huge could definitely hide in there, among all the trees. Martie blinked, then shook her head. Where on earth had that idea come from?

"All right," the math teacher said. "We're going to practice a few problems now." He wrote three on the board. "Work through these on your own, and in five minutes, we'll go over them."

Martie dutifully dug a pencil and one of her notebooks out of her bag, setting them on the desk and opening up the notebook. She quickly copied down the problems, then stuck the eraser end of her pencil in her mouth, gazing out the window to think.

The girl from the bathroom was outside the window.

Martie dropped her pencil. It clanked against the wood of her desk and then off, though it made no noise when it hit the carpet. She looked away, to see where it had gone, and when she looked back, the girl had disappeared.

"Two minutes," the teacher said.

Martie forced herself to focus on the math problems, though her thoughts kept straying back to the window. Had she really seen someone outside? Maybe it was just a reflection. There was no way someone could be outside, not here, on the second floor. There were no balconies or anything.

But even as she tried to rationalize it, she rejected the idea. The girl was wearing a long white dress, which no one here would be wearing. Everyone was in some combination of the school uniform. And her eyes were lost in shadows, if she had any at all.

Martie shook her head and put the entire thing out of her mind. Math first.

"Time's up!" The teacher stood from his desk, which was almost identical to Mrs. Weissman's, and walked back up to the whiteboard. As he began going over the first problem, Martie darted a glance out the window, but now there was only trees.

It was an old building, like Hayden had said. This building was probably older than the other ones, since those had been built for the school and this was the original home. But maybe…maybe "it's an old building" was a code for "it's haunted."

No. Ghosts weren't real. Putting everything out of her mind, she focused on her teacher, and on trig, and was pleased when she'd done all three problems correctly.

After math, there was science, up on the third floor—"So if we blow anything up, it doesn't take out anything major above it," Hayden said—near the end of the wing, where there was an open staircase and no doors to worry about. Martie hadn't gotten up the courage to ask if Hayden had seen anything out the window. Maybe she hadn't seen anything out the window, either. Maybe it was all, uh, trauma or something.

Trauma from what?

Martie got a glimpse of something, a feeling of flying, but it was gone as soon as it'd come.

Her science teacher, a Mr. Brooks, handed her a study guide as well, further disproving Mrs. Weissman's statement. Like math, this was familiar territory, and like history, it was only the tenth-grade students. Sinclair, luckily, kept to herself in the corner of the room, and there was no continuation of the previous conversation, though Martie did catch Sinclair watching her, eyes narrowed.

Class again packed up with no noticeable sign. Martie really needed to get some clarification on that.

"If you would wait a minute, Martina," Mr. Brooks said. "I'd like to have a word."

Hayden mouthed, "I'll wait in the hall," and disappeared outside.

Mr. Brooks was probably in his early forties, his blond hair just starting to be streaked with gray, and he had wide, hazel eyes that made him look friendly. "How are you holding up?" he asked, once the classroom had emptied. "I know this can all be a bit strange when you're not used to it."

Martie shrugged. "I'll get used to it. It's nice to have this opportunity."

Mr. Brooks laughed warmly. "I see you've mastered the political line. But don't feel you have to use it on me. You'll use those skills in other classes, but I prefer to maintain an environment where my students can be honest with me. And with themselves. Where they don't have to wear the mask they've created."

It sounded nice, but Martie doubted that many people actually took him up on that. "Okay, thank you, sir. I'll remember that." She straightened her bag on her shoulder. "Anything else?"

Mr. Brooks frowned slightly, staring at her intently. Martie squirmed. "Martina," he said, "I want you to know that if you need help, or someone to talk to, I'm here for you. Scholarship students don't always fare so well here, and I want to make sure you feel supported so that you can be successful."

Great, that echoed what Sinclair had said earlier. But Martie would be successful. She had to be. "Thank you, sir."

"Go on. I bet you're hungry." Mr. Brooks made a shooing motion toward the door.

Martie didn't wait.

Hayden was waiting for her in the hall. Man, Martie had really lucked out, getting her for a roommate. None of the other kids in their grade had even introduced themselves. There was some chatting before a class got started, but when class was over, everyone vacated like the room was on fire. It was weird, honestly.

"Why doesn't anybody talk after class?" Martie asked Hayden as she caught up to her.

Hayden straightened her bag. "Oh, we're not supposed to. Timeliness is of the essence, as Mrs. Weissman would say, so we're supposed to go to wherever we need to be, and then we can relax there if we have time."

Sure, that made as much sense as anything. "Thanks for showing me around and everything. I really appreciate you staying with me."

Hayden blinked, looking surprised. "I mean, why wouldn't I? Anyway, I'll show you where the cafeteria is in this building, and we can get some lunch."

That was another thing that was just plain weird about this school. Each dorm had a cafeteria in the basement, and then there was another, larger one here in the main building where everyone had lunch, and sometimes they'd do special events in it. But…why? Why not just have the one in the main building? Or the ones in the dorms? It just felt redundant.

Martie dug her map out of her portfolio. "Where is it? There are only classrooms on this."

"Oh, yeah, that thing." Hayden rolled her eyes. "I don't know why they keep giving people that." She tapped on the blackened-out wing on Martie's map. "Cafeteria's on the first floor here. Second floor is the library and archives. Third floor is old servant's quarters and off-limits to students. I think the teachers have offices or lounges or something up there."

"The cafeteria takes up the whole wing?"

"Well, no. I mean, it is pretty big, but I don't think it can be the whole wing. The library is much bigger, so there's got to be something else down there, but I don't know what it is. Kitchens, maybe." Hayden shrugged. "Anyway, let's go. Monday they have mashed potatoes, and the boys will eat them all if you're not careful."

She bounded off toward the main staircase in the middle of the building. Martie followed, folding the map back into her portfolio pocket. The floor creaked behind her, and Martie turned, expecting to see another student.

But it wasn't. It wasn't anyone. Or, at least, not anyone that she could see.

Suddenly chilled, Martie grabbed onto her bag's strap and ran to catch up with Hayden.

Chapter Three

THE REST OF THE DAY went fine, she guessed. After lunch, she had her language arts class, which was most of the sophomores once more, again around an oval table with an absurd amount of debate, and then geography, and finally programming. Apparently this last period was an elective period.

Programming was fine and all; she just wished she knew what the options were, in case there was something better. Would she be able to choose her elective for the next semester? Did anyone get to choose their electives?

No foreign language, either, which was strange. Back home, everyone had harped on how great it was to be able to speak another language, and she was pretty sure a couple of years of some language was required at the state level. Martie had been taking Russian, because it wasn't your standard Spanish/French/Mandarin, and because she had absolutely no idea where she would ever use it, aside from if she became a spy and hung out in Eastern Europe a lot.

It was an idea, after all. She had that mystery complexion.

"Oh, we do foreign language intensives," Hayden said as they headed back to the dorm after the elective period. "A week where we do several hours a day, watching movies and reading and just absorbing things. Once a quarter, maybe? The idea being that immersion is a more useful technique for learning a language than rote memorization."

Hm. Well, that was bonkers, but whatever. It probably was exciting to be doing something different than the normal routine.

As Hayden had predicted, Martie had been assigned an extracurricular fitness class, which, in her case, was martial arts. Her schedule didn't specify which martial art, just that it was immediately after the school day on Mondays, Wednesdays, and Fridays. Hayden did dance on other days.

"I could still come with you, if you'd like," Hayden said. She took off her school sweater and put on a sweatshirt that said "Good Vibes" across the front. "Show you around, make sure you don't get lost."

According to the map that had been included with Martie's acceptance letter, the rec center was behind the main school building, but on the far side, closer to the boys' dorm. The teachers' dorm was between here and there, but Martie didn't really see how she could get lost. The school wasn't that big, and the paths that led off into the woods were on the edges of the property, where she had no intention of going. No reason to go anywhere near the trees, and whatever the hell lurked in them. "No, no, I'll be okay." No reason to drag Hayden across campus in the cold when she didn't have any reason to be there. Martie could be a good friend, too.

She'd brought some of her clothes from home, but not a lot, both because she'd been told that she'd be supplied with school clothes and that she wouldn't have a lot of room. Besides, with her allowance, she could buy anything she needed. She had brought some exercise clothes—an older pair of joggers and a crop top—but as she pulled them out, she noted how crummy they looked. What had she been thinking? Still, there was nothing for it right now. Also, depending on the martial art, maybe they'd give her a gi so it wouldn't matter anyway.

She threw a cardigan over the top of her clothes and headed out, leaving Hayden bent over a book. The floor squeaked and creaked all the way down until she was outside. It was already getting dark. Must have to do with where they were in the time zone, or something, or their latitude. Martie gathered her cardigan closer, but it did little against the chill in the air. She'd check her email when she got back, see if Ms. Molina had sent over the list of things to buy. And then what? Did Ms. Molina order the things for her? Did she have a bank account or something she could access whenever?

Maybe Hayden had a coat she could borrow in the meantime. If one would fit.

The paths around the back of the school were cobblestone as well. Still clutching at her cardigan, Martie hurried around the corner of the school and past the teachers' dorm, which was a carbon copy of the girls' dorm. Some of the lights were on in the upper windows. Maybe the inside was laid out differently. That would make sense—surely they didn't make the teachers share rooms. Maybe they actually had windows. Lucky bastards.

The rec center, however, was obviously a much newer building. Like, brand new. It didn't match the other buildings architecturally at all, nor did it have the red, white, and black coloring. Instead, it was single story, mostly glass, all angles and straight lines. Inside, everything was bright white, from the walls to the tile flooring to the counters. Any metal was brushed nickel. It was like walking into a bathroom in a home décor magazine.

There was a place to scan her ID at the front desk, and an attendant pointed her in the direction of her class. Where did the non-teacher staff live? Did they have to drive all the way back to whatever town every night? Oof, that would suck.

Despite the exterior, the building was actually two stories. When Martie peeked down the staircase, she could see exercise machines, both weight and cardio. Upstairs had several classrooms, the floor type varying from room to room, the locker rooms, a small gym with basketball nets hanging from the ceiling, and a pool. Aside from being new and very bright, it didn't look all that special. Nothing she wouldn't have at home.

No massage therapist or spa services, at least not that she could see. Maybe you had to request them specially.

Martie's class was near the end of the row, with a spongy blue floor and a mirror across the entire front of the room. Eight other students were there, only one of whom she recognized from her own grade.

And, of course, that one person was Sinclair.

Martie took a deep breath. Sure, she'd gotten off on the wrong foot with Sinclair, but aggravating her was only going to make things harder. And things were already hard enough. If she wanted to survive where apparently others had failed—and she should really follow up on that—she needed allies, not enemies.

"Hey," she said, walking up to where Sinclair was stretching her arms over her head. "I wanted to apologize for the gas station thing earlier."

Sinclair was wearing a gi. It was black and had no ornamentation. Without replying to Martie, she bent over and touched the floor behind her feet.

Oh well. Baby steps, she guessed. The instructor stood near the front of the room, watching everyone stretch. She was a small Asian woman, wearing the same gi as everyone else. She stared at Martie as she approached, then, without a word, beckoned for Martie to follow her to a closet off on the side of the room. She selected a uniform from several unlabeled piles and handed it to Martie, then indicated the locker room across the way.

Okay. Maybe talking wasn't allowed in this class. Martie took the uniform and stepped into the locker room. It seemed like a fairly standard locker room, though there were nice, fluffy towels available, as well as lotion and other toiletries, and someone had placed freshly-cut flowers by the sinks.

She set the gi on a bench by the lockers, shrugged off her pants, and pulled on the uniform ones. They fit perfectly. Nice. An impressive skill, to be able to get the right size just by looking at someone. Martie opened one of the lockers and stuffed her pants in, then slid off her top and stuck that in, too. Her key card she kept around her neck as she hurriedly started to put on the gi top.

The lights overhead flickered.

Martie paused, the gi top half on. The lights flickered again, wildly, like there was a wild storm outside and they were going to lose power.

The old building excuse wasn't going to fly here.

Martie hurriedly shut the locker and finished tucking in her pants, tying her belt as she half-ran back toward the entrance of the locker room. The lights flickered again, and something moved, just out of the corner of her eye, but she didn't stop to see what—or who—it was.

Outside, in the hallway, the lights were steady. Martie went straight back into the classroom without pausing. There were more kids in the class now, twelve or so, though they were all still stretching. The instructor nodded once as Martie entered the classroom before immediately starting in on a warm-up routine.

Moving her body helped calm her down and focus her mind on other things. No one talked throughout the class, so maybe Sinclair hadn't been ignoring her after all. There was a rhythm to class—the instructor would hold up her hand, then run through a routine or a move. Then the class copied her. Before too long, the class was over.

Martie still didn't know what martial art they were doing. Some of it reminded her of the taekwondo back home, but there were only so many ways to punch and kick things.

Most kids had set their stuff along the back wall, so they just retrieved their shoes, coats, and water bottles and headed out. Still not talking. At what point were you allowed to start talking again? The hallway? The front entrance? Outside?

Okay. Maybe she could quickly grab her stuff out of the locker. Just run in, pull on some shoes and grab her stuff, and come back out to where there were other people. Or maybe someone else had gone in, so she wouldn't be alone in there.

Martie forced herself to open the door and step inside the locker room. The lights were steady. Nothing was out of place. Everything was fine as she walked across the room. Everything stayed normal as she opened the locker and pulled out her clothes and shoes. Nothing moved as she turned and started back toward the door.

Good. Martie took a deep breath. Maybe it had just been the electricity. Bad connection, being out here on top of a hill with no other civilization for miles. Tree roots growing into the wires.

Martie reached for the door handle.

The lights went out.

Martie's heart hiccupped in her chest. Tree roots in the wires. Just tree roots in the wires. Her hand closed around the door, and she pulled.

The door stuck, like it was locked.

Panic flared at the edge of Martie's vision. No way this door would be locked. It hadn't been locked a minute ago. Did it…even lock?

Okay. Okay. Martie forced several shuddering breaths in and out. There had to be another way out, right? There was a pool, so there must be a back way out of this place. She just needed to, you know, feel along the wall until she found her way all the way around. Or turn and head across the room, hands out so she didn't run nose first into something.

There was a perfectly reasonable explanation for the lights going out. Trees in the wires. Roots in the electricity.

Martie shook the doorknob a few more times before slowly taking a step back and letting go. She turned, putting one hand out in front of her, until she thought she was pointing in the right general direction. Trying not to think of what—or who—was lurking in the dark, she stepped into the room, using the other hand to clutch her clothes and shoes to her chest.

The emergency lights flashed on, casting the room in red light. In front of her, on the mirror, someone had scrawled "GET OUT." Whatever they'd used dripped down the mirror, dark and vibrant against the red of the lighting.

Martie stumbled, her back hitting the door behind her. She fumbled for the handle, but the door still wouldn't open.

"I'm trying," she whispered. "I'm trying to get out."

The emergency lights flickered, just like the normal ones had, and the girl was there, standing in between Martie and the mirror. She didn't move, and Martie couldn't see her expression, her face lost in shadow. She wore the same, long white dress that she had earlier in the day, which flowed around her in a breeze that Martie could not feel. Her hands hung down by her sides.

Martie fumbled with the door again, and this time, miraculously, it pulled open. Stumbling through it, Martie found herself back in the hallway, lights on, people going about their business like nothing was wrong.

Unable to help herself, Martie turned back to the locker room, but the lights were on there, too, and the mirror was clean.

Pausing only to slide her shoes back on, Martie ran all the way back to the dorm, her mind reeling. Who was the girl, and what did she want? Was she really…was she really a ghost? Or just someone playing an elaborate trick?

And, either way, why were they picking on Martie? She'd just gotten here—she hadn't had time to piss anyone off yet.

Well, except Sinclair. And she hadn't even done that herself. It was the whole scholarship thing.

What was it Sinclair had said? None of the scholarship students had lasted, so Martie wouldn't either.

She'd assumed it was the stress of dealing with a high-pressure school while being the only person who hadn't come from wealth. But maybe it was more than that.

Maybe no scholarship student ever lasted because someone—or something—was determined to scare them off.

Chapter Four

A HAND FELL ON Martie's shoulder. Martie yelped, but it was just Hayden.

Hayden held up both hands. "Hey, are you okay? You've been jumpy since yesterday."

God, that was an understatement. Nowhere was safe. Martie had seen the girl in every building she'd been in, which meant that she probably had full run of the school, ghost or not. Which meant she could show up at any moment. So, yeah, her nerves had seen better days.

Something else had happened recently that had also had her nerves on edge, but she couldn't seem to recall what it was. Just…bright lights? Grass? Well, if it was important, it would come to her.

Martie turned in her seat from where she'd been writing an email to Ms. Molina, asking for jackets of various warmths, hats, and gloves, as well as snow boots, since snow was a thing. In theory. "Hey," she said, pulling down her sleeves. "The whole light flickering thing—it's not just that the buildings are old, is it?"

Hayden shifted her weight. "Well, uh, they do say the school is…" She trailed off, fidgeting with the bottom of her shirt, as if saying the word was going to make it true.

Martie fiddled with the edge of her skirt as well. "Have you…have you ever seen anything?"

"It's hard to say." Hayden pulled her own chair over and sat down heavily. "Sometimes you notice something, and it's weird, right? But it's not definitely anything. A weird noise here, something out of the corner of your eye there. Maybe it's…something. Maybe it's your imagination. You know?"

"Have you ever…" Martie trailed off, Hayden's obvious nervousness rubbing off on her. But if things were already this bad, could they get worse? "Have you ever seen a girl?"

Hayden paled. "A girl?"

"Yeah, like, our age? Wearing a white dress. Or a nightgown, maybe?" Martie frowned, trying to remember a clearer image, but thinking about yesterday made her want to vomit. She couldn't recall skin or hair color. Maybe the girl hadn't had any. Maybe she'd been washed out of all her color, and that's why her dress had looked white, too.

"A nightgown?" Hayden stood, crossing to her closet. She opened it, rustled around inside, and pulled something out.

It was the identical long, white dress.

Martie stood without realizing what she was doing. "Where did you get that?"

"Everyone gets one, their first holidays here. Well, I mean, all the girls get one. You'll get one, too." Hayden looked a bit like she was going to vomit as well. "It's been tradition since the school opened, I understand. Same design and everything."

"So everyone has one?" Martie reached out to touch the nightgown. It was soft, linen maybe, with ruffles at the chest, shoulder, and wrist. "So whoever she is...she is, or was, a student here."

"Are you sure she's..." Hayden trailed off again, then returned the nightgown to the closet.

Martie had thought long and hard about that. The bathroom the morning before—well, it was weird that she hadn't been behind Martie when she'd turned, and that Martie hadn't seen or heard her run off. But it wasn't inconceivable. And the locker room yesterday, well, if someone had held the door shut from outside, and someone else had control of the lights, it definitely could have been someone alive. They could have written on the mirror while the lights were off, and then come out to stand in front of the mirror when the lights went out again. And someone could have quickly wiped the mirror off while Martie fled the room.

But standing outside the window on the second floor? There was nothing to stand on. No ledges, not even any sort of real decoration, aside from some fancy woodwork above the window. It still wasn't impossible, not if someone was motivated enough, but it got difficult. Rappelling off the roof or standing on a cherry-picker or something. Something noticeable. Sure, everyone would be in class and not outside to see, but people on other floors would notice something outside, Martie was pretty sure.

"I mean, how do you know for sure?" she asked instead of answering. "It can always be something else."

"Yes," Hayden agreed, too quickly. "Always can be."

"But all the same, will you...stick with me today?" Martie gathered her school supplies back into her bag. "She hasn't shown up when anyone else is looking."

"Absolutely." Hayden zipped her own bag closed before throwing her arms around Martie for a quick, tight hug. "Oh, don't forget your laptop. I'm 100 percent sure we're going to need them for history today."

That sounded promising, not. Martie slid hers into the special pocket for it in her bag and headed out behind Hayden. Their room automatically locked behind them and, while the floors creaked like they always did, the lights stayed steady.

Later, as they approached the school building, Martie stared upward. Definitely no ledges and, to be honest, the roof theory wasn't looking too good. It seemed fragile, for lack of a better word. No good places to anchor.

Hayden followed her gaze, brow furrowed. "What are we looking at?"

"Nothing. Never mind."

It was just as well that Hayden was sticking with her, as she didn't remember how to get to the history room. Which made sense, she guessed, since she'd come from the office yesterday instead of straight there. Now that she was here at the right time, it was relatively busy. Not terribly busy, there weren't enough kids for that, but enough that you could tell it was a school. Still weird, that they hadn't expanded. The school building was definitely big enough to fit two, three times more people. The dorms were probably the limiting factor—each could hold exactly thirty people, ten on each floor—but the top of the hill that the school occupied was large enough to build a couple more. And even if it wasn't, there was literally nothing around the hill except forest.

Why not cut some of it down and expand the school that way?

Well, not that any of that concerned her.

Mrs. Weissman stood just outside her door as they approached, holding the door open and nodding at students as they entered. Had she taught her entire career here, at Greyson, or had she only come later, once she was a more experienced teacher? If she'd been here for a while, she could be a valuable resource.

"Good morning, Mrs. Weissman," Martie said as they got close, careful to use the correct pronunciation of the teacher's name, as well as her best student voice. "I was wondering if you knew a lot about the history of the school."

Hayden gave her a weird look, but shrugged and kept going into the classroom.

Mrs. Weissman frowned even further than her normal expression. "It depends on what you're interested in, Miss Torsney. I don't tend to keep track of the more…gossip paper type of information."

What was a gossip paper? Anyway. "Has anyone ever died at the school? Like, a student?"

"You're new, so I will give you a pass," said Mrs. Weissman in a voice that said she was definitely judging Martie, "and I don't know who has been telling you things, but no. There are no records of any students dying on campus."

"But off campus?"

"Are you coming into class, or are you going to continue wasting my time with this line of inquiry?"

Martie went into class.

She didn't know why she'd expected anything useful. Mrs. Weissman was obviously trying to make everything as hard as humanly possible, so getting a straight answer out of her was no doubt a miracle.

Martie settled down in the same seat as she had before. Right. Time to make friends, or at least people who wouldn't want to potentially prank her into thinking a ghost was following her around campus. She closed her eyes for a moment, straightened her sleeves, then turned to the girl in the hijab next to her. "Hi, I wanted to formally introduce myself. I'm Martie. Does your family live close to here? Mine's in Arizona." She'd found that it helped to offer a tiny bit of personal information and ask a question when talking to someone new, because it came wrapped up with a potential topic of conversation.

The girl darted a glance across the table at Sinclair, but she was staring at her nails with a bored expression and not paying any attention. The girl relaxed, then smiled at Martie. "I'm Noor. We're from California."

"Oh, interesting. Why come to school out here, then?"

"Well, you really can't argue with the school's results." Noor folded her hands on the table in front of her. "All the best boarding schools seem to be out here on the East Coast, for some reason. Probably because the cities are older, or people just came over from Europe and started doing the same thing they'd been doing over there."

"But why do a boarding school at all?" This was something that had interested Martie. When she'd gotten her surprise acceptance in the mail, she hadn't even realized there were boarding schools in this country. That was something you read about in books set in, oh, England. Or in historical novels. And, like, she was essentially an orphan, so while Aunt Jessica might feel bad about having Martie all the way across the country for school, she probably wasn't losing any sleep over it. No one was missing Martie, and Martie wasn't missing anyone. Well, not any more than she would have anywhere.

But why, if you had a family, would you leave them for months at a time?

Noor shrugged. "Oh, you know. My parents are very busy, and I didn't see them much anyway. If I'm going to essentially be raised by the housekeeper, I might as well spend my time at one of the most prestigious schools there is, right?" She smiled brightly, and Martie smiled back.

But, wow, what a different experience. She pictured Noor in some big house up on the mountains above Los Angeles, the walls all made of glass so she could look out on the view whenever she wanted. But the house was sterile and empty, and the housekeeper had other things she needed to do, so she wouldn't be able to give Noor much attention.

Noor was probably an only child. Some trophy child, something expected, but just one, to keep up appearances and show off when they'd done well.

Martie was an only child as well, of course, but her house back in Arizona was always loud. Her dad worked from home, designing buildings and sometimes selling them, and there were periods of time when he had no commissions and would start projects around the house instead. So many projects. So many unfinished projects, and, now, they would never be finished.

No. No. She couldn't focus on that, not right now. Someday, sometime, she would have time to mourn. But not yet.

Right now, she needed to focus.

"How—" Martie started, but Mrs. Weissman lumbered to the front of the room, and all conversation died off.

"You'll see a question I've written on the board." She pointed to it with a long, wooden pointer, as if it were not obvious. "You have twenty minutes to write a response to this question, at which time we will go over your responses and discuss them for the remainder of the time period." All this was delivered in the monotone of something that had been said many, many times. "You may work on paper or on your laptop, and you may use the Internet for research as long as you vet your sources."

Hayden met Martie's eyes from across the table and raised her eyebrows a couple of times as she exaggeratedly removed her laptop from her bag. Martie rolled her eyes good naturedly and did the same.

The question on the board said, "What were the differences and similarities between the administration of the Roman and Han empires, and how did these contribute to the overall success of both?"

Martie knew very little about either, but Hayden had shared some notes with her the evening before and shown her some of the article websites Mrs. Weissman had mentioned.

"There's honestly not that much information," Hayden had said. "I'm not 100% sure Mrs. Weissman isn't writing a paper on the subject herself and is having us do some of the work for her."

Martie opened a document and dutifully copied down the question. Then she made two columns, one for the Roman Empire and one for the Han Dynasty. Then, having reached the limit of what she knew, she turned to the Internet.

Administration meant government, right? Like, how things were run. Martie opened a search engine and typed in "Roman Empire administration." Then she opened up a second window and entered "Han Dynasty administration." Both popped up numerous results on appropriate-sounding history websites. Martie should probably "vet" them somehow, however one was supposed to do that, but she didn't see how she was going to manage to vet her sources, read the information, figure out similarities and differences, and come up with a response summarizing everything, all in twenty minutes. That was term paper sorts of madness.

Still, she opened a few webpages and scanned through them. One of them was probably not a vetted source, since it had ads about the "Truth About Aliens" and "What the Government is Hiding from You" along the side of the page. Martie went to close it, when one of the ads caught her eye.

Protect Yourself from Ghosts and Other Paranormal Entities

Martie's finger paused. That was probably as whacked out as the other stories on this site, but if you'd asked her before she arrived at this stupid hilltop, she would have said ghosts weren't real, either. Maybe they weren't real, and it was all a hoax someone was running, but if it wasn't…

Martie clicked.

The article recommended staying calm, realizing ghosts meant you no harm, and calling in a local paranormal group. What the heck was the paranormal group going to do? Martie had watched enough ghost shows over the years to know that either they didn't find anything, or they riled up the spirits and made everything worse. They never seemed to do anything to deal with the problem, aside from maybe doing some sort of cleansing.

A cleansing was an option, she supposed, but the school was really, really big. It was one thing to burn sage or whatever around a house, but you'd need a whole bunch of sage even to do the dorm. Maybe a priest or something?

Martie tried to picture asking Ms. Molina for permission for a priest to bless the entire school. Yeah, no. No way that was going to happen.

A different article recommended praying to the Archangel Michael for protection or building a mental shield by imagining a colored bubble surrounding yourself. Hm. Some people did swear by the power of believing, but Martie hadn't been raised with religion and the idea of a bubble, mental or not, didn't seem terribly reassuring. Still, she supposed it wouldn't hurt to try. She opened a separate document and started a list.

The other articles she looked at reiterated what she'd already read, but added in using a protective talisman, like the Hand of Fatima, a hand with an eye in the center of it, or one of a number of different crystals that had protective qualities. Another said that the Egyptians had worn dark eye make-up to protect themselves from evil spirits—probably against the school dress code—or recommended eating copious amounts of garlic.

"It's a ghost, not a vampire," Martie murmured.

"What?" Noor asked.

"Five minutes," Mrs. Weissman called from where she lurked behind her desk.

Oh, crap. Martie quickly saved and minimized her ghost list and turned her attention back to the administration of ancient empires. By the time Mrs. Weissman rose and headed back to the table, Martie had managed about four points for each and had vaguely color-coded a couple of different aspects. Not her best work. A peek at Noor's laptop showed she'd put together several paragraphs.

However, the good news was that Mrs. Weissman did not actually collect their work, and Martie was able to make a few decent points during the discussion. She noted Sinclair watching her with narrowed eyes at the other end of the table. Maybe trying to intimidate her into submission, but whatever. Martie had bigger problems.

Actually, if the haunting was an elaborate hoax, Sinclair might be a good candidate for the mastermind. Though it wouldn't explain the whole none-of-the-scholarship-students-ever-lasted thing. Martie should really look into that. Probably best not to take that at face value.

On the way to math, Martie stuck close to Hayden but, if anything, the school felt...normal? Like, her nerves were on edge, but there was nothing to back up that feeling, no feeling of impending doom or anything.

Maybe it had been some sort of hazing test, and she'd passed because she was still here and hadn't run off campus screaming or something. Or, uh, ghosts needed energy, right? Maybe the girl had used all hers up.

Once they reached the math classroom, Martie sat on the other side of Hayden, away from the window, and purposefully did not look that way the entire class.

And nothing happened. The tension in Martie's shoulders started to drain away. It was a beautiful autumn day, and she'd probably overreacted. Or maybe it had just been stress getting to her. After all, she was in a new part of the country, at a new school, away from what family she had left, and there was the added pressure to not do anything that got her scholarship taken away. That was a lot of stress, and she'd heard that sometimes being stressed or tired could cause hallucinations.

Feeling much better, Martie gathered up her math supplies and followed Hayden to chemistry. Hayden pointed out people as they went, mentioning names and interesting facts, almost all of which Martie immediately forgot. But she had time. There were only sixty kids here, so she'd get to know all of them eventually.

She didn't know what it was that made her pause and look over her shoulder, but there, at the end of the hallway, was the girl. Her face, like always, was in shadow, and her hair and dress moved with the nonexistent breeze. Martie grabbed for Hayden's arm, unable to look away.

Get out, she barely made out, like a half-heard whisper in her head.

And then the girl...faded away, like smoke dissipating in the wind.

Well, shit.

Chapter Five

"YOU DIDN'T SEE HER?" Martie hissed to Hayden. It was mid-chemistry, and they were partnered in the back, in theory working on an experiment. In reality, Hayden was doing the experiment, and Martie was quietly hyperventilating.

"I'm sorry, no," Hayden said for the fifteenth time, carefully measuring something out and dumping it into their beaker of something else. "I must have just missed her."

"Or she's only haunting me."

Hayden made a noncommittal noise, checking the thermometer on the beaker and jotting something down in her notes.

"I need to go to the archives." Martie adjusted her safety goggles and stared down at the experiment. "I've got to find out about the other scholarship students. I think, if I can disprove Sinclair's statement that all the other scholarship students failed, I'll feel a million times better."

"You're fixating." There was a color change happening now. Hayden made more notes.

"Can you blame me?" Rubbing her temples did nothing to help Martie's growing headache. "What if this ghost has been scaring them off? Maybe it's someone who strongly believes that only people from old money belong at this school."

"Old money?" Hayden gave her a look. "Are you listening to yourself?"

Martie took a deep breath. "I'm going to go to the archives during lunch. Will you help me?"

Hayden nodded, her attention back on their experiment. "Of course, if it'll make you feel better. Also, have you considered the possibility that someone's just messing with you?"

"She disappeared while I was looking at her."

Hayden's hands shook slightly as she measured out the next ingredient, and Martie recalled how pale she'd looked that morning when they'd been discussing things. She shouldn't be forcing this on her—it wasn't fair to scare Hayden too.

"After class," Martie said, "let's go look, okay? Maybe there's a projector or something, Scooby Doo style."

"Yeah, okay."

Martie forced herself to read over the experiment and catch back up to where Hayden was, pushing things out of her mind. There was nothing to be done right now, and when she got this whole ghost/scholarship thing cleared up, she would still need to pass her classes.

Mr. Brooks smiled at her afterward. "Doing okay, Martina? I know it's early days, but remember that my offer of help still stands. With anything you need."

"I'm fine, thank you." Did she look like she needed that much help?

God, she was so paranoid. He was just trying to be helpful.

"Oh, yeah, Mr. Brooks?" Hayden said in the hallway. "He's super great. Provides extra tutoring for anyone that needs it, stocks pads and tampons in case of emergencies, and even helped Jordan book a flight home when his mother was sick."

Martie didn't know who Jordan was, but so there, brain. He was just a nice guy trying to make sure she felt at home in an environment that was new and perhaps scary for her.

She led Hayden down to where she'd seen the girl in the hallway, but there was nothing there, although Martie noted there was a security camera. It was probably impossible, but she'd love to get her hands on the footage from that. Maybe if she told Ms. Molina someone was picking on her?

But what if nothing was there?

Well, there was nothing to see here. Martie turned, intending to run down and grab a quick lunch, and found Sinclair standing in the hallway behind her.

"I have a very important question for you," Sinclair said, her face serious.

Oh, maybe Sinclair thought they'd gotten off on the wrong foot too. "Yeah?"

"Do you have any records of mental illness? Because you've been acting kind of crazy." Sinclair laughed shortly, then mimed spinning around to look at something behind her. Down the hall, one of Sinclair's friends waited, and laughed as well.

Nope. Wishful thinking. "Get bent, Sinclair." Holding her head high, Martie brushed past the other girl and headed toward the main staircase, where there were no doors to weirdly shut and lock themselves. Someone followed, which was hopefully Hayden and not Sinclair, and definitely not any disappearing ghost girls.

They ate as fast as they could, and then Hayden led the way to the archives. They were in the back of the library, which took up the entirety of the second floor of the east wing of the building. Shelf after shelf of books filled the massive room, though there were breaks with tables, and a librarian was stationed just inside the door. The archives were in their own room. It was fairly large in its own right, full of boxes and books and folders of stray papers.

Hayden put her hands on her hips. "It's a mess in here. We should digitalize all this."

Martie's heart dropped. How was she supposed to find anything in here? Nothing was labeled, not in a way she could see, and there was so much of it. "Have you used stuff in here before?"

"No." Hayden peeked inside a box, then pulled out a folder. "There's got to be some sort of organization."

Did there? Maybe they just stuffed everything in here that they might need again in the future. Martie picked up a folder, flipping it open. It was full of black and white class pictures, taken out in front of the school building. She flipped the first one over to find "1920" written on the back in pencil, but no other information. Flipping it back over, she scanned the people in the photo for the ghost girl, but the faces were not distinct, and Martie wasn't sure she'd recognize the girl anyway.

"I'm going to go get the librarian," Hayden said, dropping her folder back into the box.

Martie turned from her own folder. "Wait—"

But the door was already swinging shut behind Hayden.

Martie clutched the folder to her chest, glancing around the room. It was quiet—almost too quiet, and it felt like someone else was still in here, waiting and watching.

"Who are you?" Martie whispered to thin air. "And what do you want?"

Something whispered in the shelves around Martie. Across the room, in the back corner, one of the folders tottered on the edge of its shelf before falling onto the floor and scattering its contents.

Slowly, Martie put her current folder down and made her way across the room, stepping gingerly and slowly. But whatever had been there had gone, or had at least hidden itself back away.

Martie gathered the contents and stuck them back inside the folder before setting it down on the shelf again. But even before she'd let it go all the way, something had knocked it back onto the floor.

"All right, all right, I get the point." Martie gathered the folder back up just as Hayden and the librarian appeared.

"We don't have records specifically for scholarship students," the librarian was saying. "They're just mixed in with everyone else. You'd have to know years or names, something specific to the students."

"So there's no way to find out who was here on a scholarship?"

"Not in here." The librarian pursed her lips, staring around the room. "We really should digitalize this."

Hayden beamed. "That's what I said!"

"Is there another way to search?" Martie asked, tucking the folder behind her back. "Like, for students who didn't complete their time here for whatever reason?"

The librarian shook her head. "Nope. Everything is by year, more or less. Some of these," she pulled open the class picture folder that Martie'd had earlier, "are by type of document. But mostly it's by time. If you know what year a student was here, you can go through that stuff and find things for everyone. But if you don't know…" She shrugged. "I'd say go ask admissions, but I fear they haven't put in older records either."

Whether or not someone was here on scholarship was probably considered confidential. And something told Martie that Ms. Molina wasn't going to want to provide information on students who failed out, or ran off, or whatever, either.

"Oh," Martie said, because it felt like she should say something.

"You're welcome to look around," the librarian said. "Sorry they're not better organized. But, hey, if you need a service project or an extracurricular activity, you might consider digitalizing this. We could make an online database and make things cross-referenceable based on year, people included, type of document..." She smiled dreamily. "Oh, that would be a treasure trove."

"We'll definitely consider it," Hayden replied. "Thank you for your time."

"Oh, of course. Well, good luck." The librarian let herself out.

Hayden turned back to Martie and sighed. "Should we get more food?"

"Let's look for a little longer. Maybe we'll get lucky."

Hayden grumbled something under her breath, but she did take a box down off a shelf.

Martie moved deeper into the far corner. Kneeling on the ground, she opened the folder, spreading out the innards. There were some pictures, some notes that looked like they might be records of some sort, a couple of newspaper articles. There was nothing on the folder itself to indicate what the contents were supposed to be.

Search Called Off for Missing Student read the headline on one of the newspaper clippings. Martie picked it up to read more.

"A search for missing Greyson Preparatory Academy student George Miller was called off earlier this morning. George Miller was last seen on the campus of the remote school last Monday, the 11th, around supper, but he never returned to his room that evening, according to his roommate. George, a rare scholarship recipient, was in his fourth and final year of schooling and had been doing well. He was well-liked by his peers, and his grades were satisfactory. No one has come forward to say they had noticed anything peculiar in George's manners leading up to his disappearance.

"However, as of this morning, the staff of the academy say they have reason to believe that George has run off to join the war effort. A letter was produced to that effect, hidden among George's belongings and addressed to his roommate. Those close to George are not surprised by this decision, as they say George had good morals and liked to do what was right, though they did express some worry about why George did not tell anyone before leaving and, indeed, seems to have taken barely anything with him. It is uncertain how George left the campus and whether anyone aided him."

The article had been cut out completely, so it was unclear when it was from. Martie set it down and picked up a set of loose-leaf papers. They were faded, but the paper had not yet gone crisp, like very old papers did. There was a date on top—November 3rd—but no year, and had been torn out of a notebook.

"Dear Diary," the first line read, "I have finally arrived at Greyson Academy! It is everything I had hoped for and more, and it is so nice to be out of my foster household and someplace stable! This last place has been the worst—so many children shoved in that stupid, dilapidated house, and no adult supervision at all. They're just doing it for the money from the government, and Lord knows none of us children are seeing any of it! I was so pleased when the scholarship letter arrived and delivered me. I wonder who nominated me? I bet it was Mr. Donaldson. He was always so sweet, though I'm not sure he wasn't hitting on me. Gross, right?"

Martie's blood ran cold. This person had also just gotten their scholarship acceptance out of nowhere. That was a weird way to run a school, to accept people for scholarships without any forewarning that someone had nominated them or that they were under consideration. Martie set the letter down and turned to the pictures. There were only three. One was of a young man, black and white, wearing a much more formal uniform than was required now. On the back, in pencil, someone had written, "George Miller, 1916," and then, farther down, "Disappeared."

The second picture was of a smiling, curly-haired redhead wearing a headband with a fabric flower on it.

This one was in color, and, if Martie had to guess, she'd put it in the 1970s. On the back, someone, but not the same someone—this handwriting was quite a bit messier—had written, "Donna Winters, 1978." And, again, down in the corner, "Disappeared."

The third was of another girl, maybe from the 1940s, sitting on the steps on the front of the school with her hands wrapped around her knees. This one was labeled "Alice Robinson, 1943," and, just like the other two, "Disappeared."

Martie sat back on her heels, realizing her hands were shaking. The librarian had said that everything was labeled by time or type of document, but obviously someone had gone through and made this file which, from first glance, seemed to be specifically about scholarship students. And, if that was the common theme, then at least three of them had disappeared. Not left the school. Not failed out.

Disappeared.

Chapter Six

MARTIE STOOD IN the first-floor corridor of the school, except it was longer and darker than normal, and the walls seemed to tip and spin, like a funhouse.

At the far end of the corridor stood the girl. Same as always, face in shadow, dress and hair blowing in a wind that didn't exist, hands dangling by her sides.

"Who are you?" Martie called. "What do you want? Why are you bothering me?"

Martie blinked, and they were outside, standing among the gravestones. The girl was much closer now, close enough that Martie could see she only had dark circles where eyes should go. Silently, the girl pointed, maybe to one of the graves on the very cusp of the hill. The gravestone listed to the left.

"What is it?" Martie asked. "Is this your grave?"

The girl continued to point. Martie took a step closer, skin crawling. The gravestone, like those around it, was white, simple, unmarked.

"I don't know what I'm supposed to see."

The girl dropped her hand, then turned, walking toward the edge of the hill. Martie followed. Beyond them, below them, more gravestones lay, and beyond them, trees and trees and trees. But there was something in the trees—something big, and dark, and searching.

Martie blinked awake, the dream fading. Above, only the faintest light shone in through the skylight. She sat up, rubbing one eye, then sighed. According to her phone, it was barely past five.

She hadn't slept well, but that was to be expected. Across the way, Hayden slept, her chest rising and falling with her breath. Martie stared enviously at her for a moment before crawling out of bed and descending to the floor. She wrapped her bathrobe—another thing a courtesy of the school—around her pajamas and sat down at her desk. She flipped her laptop open, not really sure what she was going to do with it.

She'd snuck the folder from the archives out with her, slipping it into her bag while Hayden'd had her head buried in one of the other boxes. Why had the ghost— and it must have been the ghost, right?—wanted her to find this? As far as she could figure, the ghost must be trying to scare her off. Three other scholarship students had disappeared, so she could be next.

Or it was a warning, that the ghost was coming for her, too.

She'd run all three names through her search engine already. George Miller, 1916, just came up with digital copies of the newspaper article she'd already seen, along with some other ones that must have pre-dated the one in the folder, noting how search parties with dogs had been sent into the woods.

Alice Robinson didn't come up with anything at all. Donna Winters was slightly more useful, since she was more recent than the others, enough that Martie had figured out that she was from Cincinnati and had been born in 1962. But not much else was out there, or Martie hadn't been able to find it. As far as she could tell, none of the three had ever resurfaced, nor had their remains ever been found, if something bad had happened to them.

Martie rubbed her temples. What was she supposed to do with this information? She wasn't going to run, if that's what the others had done. She needed this. She had to be successful here. That's what her parents would want.

Her parents, God. Despite this opportunity, she would give all the scholarships to all the best schools if it would bring them back.

But she couldn't. Could she? No. That was crazy.

With a sigh, Martie snapped the laptop shut again. Maybe she could…just ignore the ghost. Maybe that's where the others had gone wrong. Maybe they'd let it scare them into whatever. What was the ghost going to do if she didn't react?

A snippet of the dream that had woken her floated back, of standing in the graveyard at the edge of the hill and looking out at the trees.

That was it. The ghost lured them into the trees, into the woods, where they probably got eaten by wolves or bears or whatever the hell lived in forests and ate people. Bigfoots. Bigfeet? It didn't matter.

Well, she wasn't going anywhere near the damn trees.

She might as well get ready and do some homework before class started.

Taking one last look at Hayden—still sleeping—Martie creaked the door open. She took a step out and kicked something that had been left just outside. Whatever it was skittered across the floor, coming to a rest just on the edge of the landing. It was a small, plain box with a ribbon tied around it. Martie grabbed it from as far away from the edge as she could manage—didn't want to give the ghost any opportunities to be a little more hands-on in getting rid of a scholarship student— and untied the ribbon.

Inside was a slip of paper in a messy hand that said, "Thought this might help you." And underneath that was a brown and yellow crystal that had been made into a pendant. A silver chain sat in the very bottom of the box.

Martie picked up the crystal and stared at it. It was tiger's eye, if she wasn't mistaken, one of the crystals that was said to have protective qualities, at least according to the Internet. She slid the pendant onto the chain, then fastened it around her neck. It sat fairly low, against her sternum, so she could wear it under her uniform without it being obvious.

Wow. What a thoughtful gift. There was no name on the note, so who knew who it was from.

But apparently she'd been more obvious about the ghost than she'd thought. Oof.

Okay. She now had a protective talisman. She should be able to shower in peace.

No one was in the bathroom when she arrived, which was no surprise. No one lurked in the mirror behind her or wrote threatening messages on it. No one pulled on her shower curtain while she washed her hair, and no one touched her clothes where she'd left them folded up outside the shower.

Haha! Success!

Wrapping herself back in her bathrobe, she made her way back to her room. It was still early, and no one else was around. There were five rooms on each floor, plus a bathroom. Martie hadn't really figured out who lived where yet. Hayden probably knew. Oh well.

It was another hour before Hayden woke up. Martie had hidden the folder away again. She didn't need it, not now. She'd seen no sign of any haunting yet, and she felt better, more centered and grounded. So, instead, she'd read two chapters in the 18th century Russian novel they were working through for Classical Literature and had pre-pulled up some resources for history, as well as gone back over the notes Hayden had left her.

Everything was going her way. She was on top of the discussion in history, earning not one but two head nods from Mrs. Weissman, and the test in trigonometry at least felt like it went well. In chemistry, she and Hayden managed to get through their experiment faster than anyone else, and had the appropriate reaction as well.

"Well done," Mr. Brooks said, and winked.

Oh! Mr. Brooks had probably sent the talisman. Martie could feel it hanging heavily against her skin. He'd been so adamant about being helpful, so he'd probably seen Martie's need and had dealt with it, like he'd helped with Jordan's flight problem.

She still didn't know who Jordan was.

After class, she went up to Mr. Brooks. "I wanted to thank you for everything."

Mr. Brooks smiled. "It was nothing. I'm always here if you need anything."

Things were definitely looking up. It was already lunch, and there was no sign of the ghost girl.

There was, however, still Sinclair.

"You're chipper this morning," she said, standing behind Martie in line for food. "Did you roll out of your bed and give yourself a concussion?"

"It's a lovely day," Martie said as sincerely as she could manage. On her other side, Hayden blinked. "Why worry when there are so many things to enjoy in life?"

Sinclair frowned, then turned to Hayden. "Did she roll out of bed and give herself a concussion?"

Hayden shrugged.

"Haha." Martie brushed her hair behind her shoulders.

Sinclair narrowed her eyes.

Martie studied the lunch menu. The chicken fried steak with mashed potatoes sounded artery-clogging. She'd get that.

"Oh, man," Hayden murmured to herself. "I wish I weren't lactose intolerant. I really want some cheese."

The line inched forward. Martie relished the mundane-ness of it, basking in the sound of people chatting and eating around them.

"Fine!" Sinclair said loudly from behind her. "In Classical Literature we're going to be assigned a project that we will need a partner on. You will be my partner."

Hayden choked and started coughing.

Martie patted her on the back. "Uh, sure?"

"Excellent," said Sinclair, crossing her arms over her chest. She turned away with a huff.

Okay, weird. The line moved along, Martie retrieved her food, and she and Hayden sat down at a table in the middle of the room.

"Oh my god." Hayden dropped her tray the last half inch, knocking her silverware onto the table. "Sinclair asked you to be her partner!"

"So?"

"So?" Hayden echoed. She sat down heavily. "You must have really impressed her somehow. Everyone always wants to be her partner, and she's very picky. I don't think I've ever heard her ask someone before."

Martie shrugged, but internally, she did a little dance. Could this day get any better?

And, for a whole week, things were great. Martie introduced her entire way through the sophomore class, as well as some people in other grades who were in a few of her classes. She started to get used to the routine and quirks of the school. Ms. Molina dropped off her new cold weather gear and a debit card that would be loaded with her monthly allowance. The leaves fully blossomed into seas of reds and golds, making it look like the school's hill was afloat on a burning ocean.

At no point did Martie see the girl.

Sinclair had been right about the partner project, which was to take a question about their Russian novel, assigned by the teacher, each pick a side, and prepare notes in a debate style. Sinclair was not the easiest person to work with; she often blew off Martie's suggestions, though Martie noticed she did sometimes integrate Martie's ideas anyway, even after ridiculing them.

But this was normal, expected school problems. And she could deal with this.

Then, one Saturday morning, Hayden crawled out of bed way too early and started putting on jeans and sneakers and a shirt that had definitely seen better days. Martie watched her through one cracked eyeball.

"You're going to be late," Hayden said as she braided her long, blonde hair into a long plait.

"Late for what?"

"It's Service Day."

That answered nothing. Martie dragged herself out of bed while Hayden went to the bathroom, digging through her clothes from home and picking out the oldest ones. She hadn't really packed anything ratty, since she'd been trying to make a good impression. She was tying her shoes when Hayden returned. She tossed Martie a pair of leather work gloves and tucked her own in her back pocket. "Ugh, I wish they didn't start so early. It never takes us past lunch time anyway, so it wouldn't hurt anything to start a little later."

"Sure. What are we doing?"

"Oh. I keep forgetting you haven't been here that long. Service Day. Supposed to teach us to support our communities, that nobody, no matter how rich or important you are, is above anyone else. So once a quarter, we do maintenance tasks around the school. Sometimes it's gardening-related, sometimes it's going through old stuff and getting rid of things, sometimes it's cleaning or polishing or what have you."

Martie brushed her own hair into floofy pigtails. "Aren't there people that do some of those jobs?"

"Well, yeah, but some of this stuff never gets touched outside of Service Day. And some of it is just busy work to make sure everyone has something to do." Hayden pulled a hat on over her hair. "We'd better go, though, or they'll give our jobs away and we'll be stuck with whatever's the worst."

They ate a quick breakfast before Hayden led Martie outside. Most, maybe all, of the student body milled around in front of the school building, dressed in their Sunday Worst and all looking like they'd rather be in bed.

Mr. Brooks appeared out of the school, looking much happier than any of his charges, and bounded down the steps toward them. "Happy Service Day, everyone! We're just finalizing assignments, but you're welcome to come inside and wait until we post them."

The kids meandered inside, where it was only slightly warmer. It always felt weird, being in a school building when school was not happening, and this was no exception. The corridors were dark and empty, with the only signs of life being concentrated to the front entrance area.

Even though Martie hadn't seen the ghost in over a week, she still didn't spend any time peering into the darkness. Just in case.

A couple of the other sophomores came over to chat while the science teachers deliberated in the corner.

"I guess it is good to do something with your hands," Noor said, looking like she didn't believe it, "but I do wish they tied it in with whatever lesson better. Generally, you're assigned a job and whenever you're done, you're done, and you can just do whatever."

"It's to show that we need to take pride in the school by helping to maintain it," Charlie, a sandy-haired boy, said. "To show that community requires everyone to take a part."

"If you say so." Noor frowned down at the floor, then looked back up. "Oh, hey, Martie, we're going to do an anime night in the cafeteria tonight. You should come."

"Which anime?"

Martie never got her answer, though, because the science teachers finalized their decisions and hung the assignments up on the window of the main office. Immediately, everyone crowded around, trying to see their names and their assignments. Martie went along with them, not wanting to be left behind, lest she get the worst assignment, and also not wanting to spend any time lingering in case she saw something she didn't want to down one of the darkened corridors.

There were four lists, one for each grade, and then they were alphabetical by last name. Martie found her name easily enough.

But the assignment beside it—*Prune the landscaping around the graveyard*—made her blood run cold.

No. No. She'd sworn to herself that she wouldn't go over there, that she wouldn't let the ghost lure her into the forest like she'd lured the others before her. There had been no conceivable reason for her to ever go over there.

Trying to remain calm, she nudged Hayden in the arm. "Hey, do you want to switch?"

Hayden stared at her like she was crazy. "Why on earth do you want to switch? The graveyard's mostly maintained by the landscaper. You just clip a few branches here and there and pull up any weeds, and you're done. It'll take you an hour, tops. I'm going to be going for hours." She groaned.

Martie glanced at Hayden's assignment. *Polish the wood railings in the girls' dorm building.*

"There's so many of them," Hayden murmured. "Whoever designed those buildings was entirely too fond of staircases and open corridors." She laid a hand on Martie's arm. "Think of me fondly." She headed toward the science teachers, where she received some wood polish and a rag.

Martie took a deep breath. She knew what the ghost was trying to do, and so she'd just have to trust that she wouldn't fall for it. She, too, headed for the science teachers. Mr. Brooks smiled at her as he handed her some pruning shears and a weeder.

"Oh, you've got the graveyard too?" A tall, lanky redheaded boy was receiving his own gear from a different science teacher. "Looks like we'll be partners for today."

The fear lifted off Martie's shoulders. "Oh! Great."

She followed him out of the building and across the lawn. "I'm Winchester," he said. "Whose butt did you kiss to get this choice assignment? I helped Ms. Caradoc organize the supply room." He shuddered. "There were so many unlabeled vials growing strange things. We just threw them out, but I'm not sure that we didn't break some sort of hazard laws."

Martie introduced herself. "I didn't kiss anyone's butt that I know of. Maybe they just wanted to give me an easy task since it's my first time."

"Oh! You're the new scholarship student. How are you liking the school?"

Apparently everyone knew she was here on scholarship now. Joy. And school was great, if you ignored certain paranormal things which, to be fair, had tapered off. "It's a big change, but I think I'll be okay."

The graveyard loomed ahead. Martie swallowed hard. It was a gray day, clouds hiding the sun and washing out the landscape. But, still, the gravestones stood out, bright white against the grass. Martie wiped her hands on her pants.

"Still, weird that you got this your first try," Winchester was saying. What kind of name was

Winchester? His family probably had a wall full of animal heads somewhere. "Freshman, for example, normally get the worst stuff. Like, one of the jobs is to wash the towels in the rec center. I think they leave them for a few days before Service Day so there's a ton, and they've also started growing mildew. Or you could have gotten cleaning out the dumpsters."

"There's dumpsters?"

"Ha! Little do you know." He wrinkled his nose. "Do people clean those out normally? No. I think they just felt like they had to have enough jobs for everyone, so they made ones up."

They reached the edge of the graveyard. Martie lurked on the outside as Winchester stepped inside. It was worse than she'd thought up close, like the world was closing in on her. It was hard to breathe.

"Hey, you okay?" Winchester turned back toward her. "You've gone all pale."

Martie forced in a few deep breaths, which helped only slightly. "How can you just go in there? There's people under you." There were no rows, no organization. The headstones were all over the place, leaning this way and that. It was…it was a disgrace. Whoever was buried here—just like her dream, there were no names—they deserved respect, right? Not this haphazardness, where people could stomp all over them accidentally.

Winchester laughed. "Maybe. It's not like the dead are going to care if you walk on their bones." He must have seen her face, because he sobered. "Hey, look, we're doing something to help, right? By maintaining the graveyard, we're helping. Showing them that someone still cares, that we're still taking care of them."

Okay, yeah. That was a good way to think of it. They were showing respect by making sure the area was as tidy as possible. Martie still trod lightly, trying to avoid where she thought the graves were as she pulled weeds, and Winchester cut off branches that were getting too close, mostly down the side of the hill.

Something down in the woods drew her attention. She turned her head, staring down into the trees, but there was nothing down there. No movement, no wind, no sound. Yet it still felt like something or someone was watching her.

Best to get out of here as fast as possible. Focusing on her work, she refused to so much as glance in the forest's direction again.

Hayden had been right—there wasn't much to the graveyard job, especially not with two of them—and soon they were done. Relief washed over Martie as she and Winchester made their way back to the school building to return their tools. That—hadn't been bad at all. There'd been no sign of the ghost, no sign of any attempts to lure her into the forest. Her pendant must be working.

She said goodbye to Winchester, and then she was free. Maybe she should go help Hayden.

The dorm was relatively quiet when Martie stepped inside. She found Hayden on the main staircase, wiping down the railings with the attitude of someone who had been slated to be executed. Martie glanced around, but no one else seemed to be helping. "Is it just you?"

"What do you mean, is it just me?"

"I don't know, I had a partner."

"Graveyard duty, and a partner?" Hayden sat down heavily on the steps. "Where have I gone wrong?"

"I can help, if you'd like."

"Would you?" Hayden's entire countenance changed. "God, I'm so glad you're my roommate. Here, I have an extra cloth."

With Hayden spraying both her and Martie's sides of the banister, they made quick—well, quicker—work of the staircase and second floor. The staircase to the third floor was easy, since it was purely functional rather than ornate, which left just the third-floor landing.

Hayden had started humming somewhere on the second floor. She happily sprayed the railing, then headed to the far end to work back toward Martie, while Martie worked from the top of the staircase. Hayden was pretty heavy with the spray, so Martie could use the excess to do the vertical parts as well.

They met in the middle, just outside their room. Hayden wiped her sleeve across her forehead. "I can't thank you enough for doing this, Martie. In fact, I—" She cut off suddenly, her face going white.

"What? What is it?" Martie spun toward their door, heart beating, afraid of who she was going to see there.

But the ghost girl wasn't there. Instead, someone had carved, in deep gouges, "GET OUT" across the door to their room.

Chapter Seven

"THIS IS VERY serious," Ms. Molina said as she climbed the staircase in the girls' dorm. "We have a strict no bullying policy, and, of course, destruction of property is never acceptable."

Martie and Hayden crept up behind her. Martie's heart pounded in her chest. It had to be the ghost. But phantom writing on a mirror or whispers in a hallway were one thing. The doors here were solid wood, old and strong. The strength necessary to carve something into them—Martie wasn't even sure she could do it if she tried.

She felt the tiger eye crystal through her shirt. She wore it all the time, unless she was in the shower or the pool, and she still hung it outside or wrapped it in her towel so it was close. Maybe, since the ghost could no longer get to her, it had decided to use other methods.

They came up onto the third floor. Martie found herself walking closer to Hayden, or perhaps they were both huddling together. Either way, they were practically on top of each other when they came up to their door and found…

…nothing.

No carving. No "GET OUT." Just the door.

"What the—" Martie said.

Ms. Molina rounded on them. "Is this some kind of prank?"

"No!" Hayden shook her head hard enough to send her braid flying. "It was there, I swear. I took that picture that I showed you."

Ms. Molina pursed her lips, placing her hands on her hips. "A carving like the one you showed me doesn't just disappear, young lady."

Hayden squeaked some response, but Martie was no longer listening. She ran her hands down the door, but it was true. The carving was gone, as if it had never been there. That was weirder. A mirror could be wiped off—but how did you get rid of a carving?

With a sinking feeling, Martie ran her keycard past the sensor for their room. The door clicked open, and Martie pushed inside to find bedlam.

Clothing everywhere. Bedding torn apart. Both chairs on their sides in the middle of the floor. The contents of at least Martie's school bag tossed every which way.

And, on the wall, a carving that said, "Martie was here."

She must have made some noise, because Hayden and Ms. Molina stopped their conversation and came up behind her. Hayden made a keening noise in the back of her throat, and even Ms. Molina seemed speechless.

Tears pricked the corners of Martie's eyes. No. No. She didn't need this. Why couldn't she just be left alone? Hadn't she gone through enough lately?

Ms. Molina composed herself first. "I assume neither of you did this?"

"We left together this morning," Hayden said, "and only now came back."

"Can both of you confirm this?"

Hayden went pink. "I've been polishing the banisters all morning. There's cameras in the common areas, right? You can confirm that."

Martie's voice caught in her throat. She gingerly stepped into the room, picking up the stuffing from a pillow. How was she supposed to live like this, always fearing what was coming next? No wonder those other scholarship students had left. Maybe, after some time, the forest was the preferrable option.

"Martie didn't do it," Hayden was saying behind her. "She had a partner for her job, and then she came to help me with mine. Someone's trying to get her thrown out."

Ms. Molina said something in response, but Martie didn't hear it. Tears rolled down her cheeks now, and she wiped at them with her sleeve-covered forearm. It wasn't fair. She'd already lost so much. She needed this opportunity, before her life completely fell apart. If she had to go back to Aunt Jessica's and face everything she had lost...

"You said there were cameras in the common areas?" she asked, wiping her face again. She stood, turning to Hayden and Ms. Molina, the stuffing still in her hand. "We'd be able to see if someone came into our room, yes?"

"Obviously someone came into our room!"

But was it someone the camera would see? "So it will be on the cameras," she said again, not at all sure it would be.

Ms. Molina pursed her lips. "I'll look into it," she said. "And I'll send someone to help you clean this up." Her heels clicked as she headed back out toward the stairs.

"She doesn't believe us," Martie said. She dropped the stuffing in the trash, then started gathering up her clothes. Well, the clothes. She'd have to check sizes later to see what was whose. Hayden wore, like, extra extra small. But the good news is that the clothes seemed to be intact, and the sheets as well. Only the pillows had actually been ruined.

Hayden stomped inside, dropping to the ground to gather up the papers, which she began to sort into two different piles. "How rude! Of course we wouldn't do this ourselves! What would be the point?" She slammed down a few sheets of paper. "Someone's trying to frame you."

"Or scare me off." Martie stared up at the "Martie was here" carved into the wall. It, at least, did not seem to be going anywhere, but maybe only because they hadn't left. Still…it didn't quite look like the "GET OUT" on the outside of the door, like two different people had carved them.

She rubbed her temples. Maybe someone had come into their room—a real someone, someone who, like the ghost, didn't like scholarship students and wanted Martie gone. No one had been actively malicious to her, except Sinclair, but that was too obvious, right? And Sinclair had been working on that project with her.

Maybe, just maybe, Sinclair had asked to be her partner so she could sabotage Martie. But Martie didn't really see how. The way the project was set up, Martie prepared her arguments for her side and Sinclair did hers. Unless she'd somehow conspired with the teacher to give Martie the wrong question for debate—far-fetched—there was really nothing Sinclair could do to affect Martie's performance at all.

But Sinclair did know something. Not about the mess in their room, necessarily, but about the previous scholarship students. The school wouldn't tell her about them, but maybe Sinclair would.

Still, partnering for a Classical Literature project did not a friend make. And Sinclair relied so heavily on appearances.

Mr. Brooks, too, had mentioned something about things being tough for scholarship students. Martie's hand again went to her pendant. He'd been so helpful already—so maybe he'd be willing to help again.

THE WEEKEND stretched on forever. Even though neither Martie nor Hayden said anything about their room, word got around anyway. It was hard to hide the repairman who came to repair the wall, to be fair, especially since he showed up as people were trickling back in from their Service Day assignments. Ms. Molina had come by with new pillows, her lips still pursed, her manner still cold.

Opinion seemed to be divided on what had happened. Some people certainly thought that, yes,

Martie and/or Hayden had done it themselves. Others agreed with Martie that someone was trying to scare her off. One freshman had stood up Sunday morning at breakfast and launched into a long, passionate speech about how treating people poorly just because they were different was wrong, and that included socioeconomic classes as well as things like the color of someone's skin or what state they had come from. The girl's heart was in the right place, at least.

But, like all things that you desperately do not want to talk about, it was all anyone else *did* want to talk about. Martie had wanted to make the acquaintance of the other students, but not like this, not when half the people she'd never talked to before came up to her to give their opinion on the situation, especially when that opinion was so often negative.

The carving in the wall had not gone away, not like the "GET OUT" had. It was gone now, plastered over and repainted, but Martie could still picture it, each letter dug into the wall violently. It'd been over Hayden's bed, so if she lay on her side, looking over the room, it was easy to still see it there, looming.

Where had she gone wrong? Why did she deserve this? Silent, hot tears flowed into the night.

By the time Monday finally rolled around, Martie's nerves were shot. She sat quietly through history and trig, only talking when necessary. For the most part, her classmates tiptoed around her, but at least they weren't actively picking on her.

"It's not your fault," Hayden said during their experiment in chemistry. "Don't let them get to you."

Hayden had said this in a variety of combinations over the last few days, though it never seemed to help. Martie could see how she looked to a bunch of rich kids who had gotten into this school through a combination of connections, money, and good grades—like an ungrateful thug, someone who'd gotten into the school without having any of what they had, except the grades, and then didn't even appreciate their good luck.

Martie sighed.

"Besides," Hayden continued. "I'm expecting a surprise in the mail. Let's run back to our room at lunch, and I'll show it to you."

A surprise? At the same time, Martie's heart lurched at the thought of their room. This was really the first time both of them had been out of it since the incident. It had seemed prudent for one of them to guard it, so whoever had trashed the room couldn't do it again. They could return at lunch and find more things carved into the wall.

Martie nodded and turned to pick up the next ingredient for their experiment. On the countertop next to her, in the same handwriting as all the "GET OUT"'s, it said, "GIVING UP?"

As Martie watched, the words faded away.

"Martie?" Hayden asked. "You've gone white."

Something stirred, deep in Martie's gut. Giving up? No, she wasn't giving up. She wasn't going to let someone scare her—or guilt her—into leaving. She was going to stay, and she was going to thrive, and damn anyone or anything that tried to get in her way.

She picked up the ingredient and handed it to Hayden. "I'm fine. Don't worry. And I can't wait to see your surprise."

After class, she waited until the room had mostly cleared out—Hayden'd gone off to get her package—then approached Mr. Brooks' desk. He smiled, like he always did, when she approached, folding his hands on the desktop. "Martina, good morning. I heard about all the unpleasantness over the weekend. Too bad, really, after I worked so hard to get you an easy job for Service Day."

"Thank you, but you didn't need to."

Mr. Brooks flapped one hand. "Pish posh. I told you before that we seem to have a hard time keeping scholarship students, and I want to make sure you're as happy here as can be."

Martie fidgeted with the strap on her bag. "That's just it, Mr. Brooks. Can you tell me what happened to the other scholarship students?"

"What happened to them?"

"Why they didn't complete their schooling here. Why they left. If," she swallowed, "something happened to them."

The smile on Mr. Brooks' face morphed into a frown, but after a long moment, his expression evened back out. "Happened to them? Oh, Martina, you make it sound like a big conspiracy."

"Is it?"

Mr. Brooks laughed. "No, nothing of the sort. It is, as I'm sure you've noticed, somewhat hard to be the only student here who didn't buy their way in. No matter how popular one gets, or how well you get along with your classmates, there's still the idea, in the back of everyone's head, that you're different, no matter how hard everyone tries not to think about it. And sometimes, that idea becomes too much, for whatever reason. Or sometimes there was another reason. One, I believe, went to enlist, and another got pregnant and was asked to leave. There's nothing sinister about it—it's just life."

That made sense, Martie guessed, but it was still so weird that not a single one of them had completed their time here. "Has there been a lot of scholarship students?"

"You have to understand that Greyson Academy has a reputation to maintain." Mr. Brooks leaned back in his chair. "A student that does not finish, who leaves the school, is a negative mark on our record. So, no, there hasn't been a lot. It normally takes some time before the board is willing to try again after something has gone wrong."

"When was the last one?"

"Oh, it's been probably fifteen, twenty years. I wasn't here for that one, but I understand his grandmother became ill, and he went home to help her."

Surely that was an understandable reason, and surely, occasionally, non-scholarship students also left the school for whatever reason, like Hayden's previous roommate. It didn't make much sense, one way or another. Why have scholarships at all, if they hardly ever handed them out, and if they always went south in the end? From Martie's research of the school, she knew they had a waiting list, so why not just cut the scholarship program entirely and just keep to paying students?

Maybe there was some sort of law for schools, one that said you had to provide opportunities for everyone to have access to an equivalent education. But Greyson

Academy was a private school, and she was pretty sure private schools could do whatever they wanted.

"Has anyone ever died on campus?"

Like Mrs. Weissman, Mr. Brooks went through a number of expressions before settling on vague concern. "Why do you ask?"

"Well, you know."

"Do I?"

He had to know, or else he wouldn't have gotten her the pendant. Was there some reason why he couldn't talk about it? Cameras or something? Martie glanced around, but she didn't immediately see anything. "Yes?"

Mr. Brooks waited a few seconds. "Well, all right, then."

She wasn't going to get anything else out of him. He'd probably get a message to her later, like he had the pendant, when it was safe to talk, or when what he said couldn't be directly linked to him. "Have a good afternoon, Mr. Brooks."

"See you tomorrow, Martina."

She found Hayden down in the entrance, waiting for her. "Did your package come?"

Hayden patted her bag. "Yeah. Let's go back to the dorm, and I'll show you."

"Just a minute, please, ladies." The telltale clicking of Ms. Molina's heels sounded across the floor. "If you would come into my office, please."

Ms. Molina's office was one of six in the main office, which resembled what Martie would expect to find in the top floor offices of some fancypants lawyer. Thick, plush carpeting, dark wood paneling, large oil paintings showing various facets of the school and grounds. Her office was large enough for several bookcases and filing cabinets to ring the edges while still having room for the largest wood desk Martie had ever seen.

Ms. Molina gestured at two guest chairs as she closed the heavy wood door with a click. Martie sank into one, relaxing involuntarily into its comfort. This might be the nicest chair she'd ever sat in. Ms. Molina probably entertained the parents of potential students here.

Ms. Molina sat down across from them. "Ladies, I am going to give you one more chance to tell me what happened Saturday morning."

One more chance? Beside Martie, Hayden narrowed her eyes. "I beg your pardon?"

"Right, I'll get straight into it, then. We've gone over the surveillance tapes, and there is no indication that anyone, other than you two, went into your room on Saturday."

Martie took a deep breath. That wasn't a surprise, but it was disheartening. "Did the door carving show up on the recording?"

Ms. Molina shifted in her seat. "It's unclear. We can see you two approach your door and your reactions, but the door itself is not clear enough to make out details. For all I know, this was all just a show for the camera. You both obviously knew it was there."

Martie furrowed her brow. "Why would we make a show?"

"She thinks we made up the door carving, and that we trashed our own room." Hayden's voice had gone to ice.

"What? Why would we do that?" It had been hard enough to hear that theory from the other kids, but there was something worse about an authority figure believing it.

"I understand that life has been hard for you lately, Martina." Ms. Molina gave her what was probably meant to be an understanding look, but it radiated displeasure instead. "It can be natural to act out when you have experienced so much upheaval in such a short time."

Martie sputtered, but nothing came to mind to counteract this statement.

"However," Ms. Molina continued, "this sort of behavior cannot be tolerated. I'm afraid I will have to put you on probation for the rest of the semester and, if more incidents of this vein occur, we will have to pull your scholarship."

Tears stung Martie's eyes. This was wildly unfair, but what could she say? The cameras didn't show who entered their room because a ghost did it? Yeah, right, that was not going to improve Ms. Molina's opinion in any way.

"No," Hayden said.

Ms. Molina transferred her gaze to Hayden. "I beg your pardon?"

"No, you will not put Martie on any sort of probation." There was a firm, dark undercurrent to Hayden's voice that didn't sound like her at all. "I will personally swear that Martie did not do that to our room. She was not in the room while I was not there—that is confirmed through eyewitness reports and no doubt your own cameras—and the room was not in that condition when we left it Saturday morning. I don't know if someone tampered with your camera feed or not, but this was not Martie, and she will not suffer any more consequences for this."

"Miss Lambert, I don't think you—"

"No, I will not brook any discussion on this." Hayden stood, and Martie hurriedly followed her. "I do not need to tell you who my family is or what they mean to this school. If I give my word that Martie did not do this, you will respect that."

Ms. Molina pursed her lips, but after a moment, she nodded once.

Hayden lifted her chin. "You might consider who has access to your cameras and whether or not any of those people would have any reason to tamper with them and, if so, what else they are tampering with." Head held high, she turned and walked out of the office.

Martie went after her, casting one glance over her shoulder at Ms. Molina. She did not look happy. Even if she listened to Hayden and didn't level any consequences on Martie, it was clear that Martie had lost most, if not all, her respect.

It would be the same way with the other kids, the ones who thought she'd done it. They would talk, and believe, no matter what Martie did.

God, how was she supposed to fight this? She wiped at the corners of her eyes, trailing behind Hayden as she left the school building and started down the cobblestones toward their dorm.

Hayden didn't say a word the entire trip, her shoulders tensed and her hands balled into fists. She didn't even look at Martie until they reached the third floor and stood outside their room.

"I guess we should open it," Martie said. "Make sure nothing's happened while we were out."

Hayden dug out her lanyard from under her sweater and knocked her keycard against the sensor. As she pushed the door open, both she and Martie craned their heads to see inside.

Everything was as they'd left it. Martie let out a long breath.

Hayden whirled on her, and, with a cry, threw her arms around Martie's shoulders. "That's so unfair of Ms. Molina! And everyone! Picking on you over all that. I won't stand for it."

Martie blinked. "I appreciate what you said back there."

"I meant every word of it." Hayden pulled the door shut again and started digging through her bag.

"I've never...I mean, I didn't know..." Martie stopped, unsure how to articulate how poised and intimidating Hayden had been without insulting how she normally was.

Hayden smiled wryly, though, like she could sense what Martie was thinking. "Comes with the territory, I'm afraid. Wealth is power, in this world, and my parents made sure I knew how to use it when it mattered. Always makes me feel a little sick, though." She paused, cocking her head to one side. "Actually, no, not this time. I don't regret forcing her to listen to me. Oh, here it is."

She pulled an envelope out of her bag. One side had been neatly cut open, and Hayden dumped the contents into her hand. There was a sticker of a keyhole, the facsimile of a large, brass one, but that was it.

Martie furrowed her brow. "What's that for?"

"It was the girl you keep seeing, wasn't it?" Hayden tucked the envelope back into her bag, though her hands were shaking a bit now. "That's who trashed our room, and that's why they didn't show up on the camera."

Martie thought of the way her clothes had been thrown about her very first morning, when she'd seen the girl in the mirror, but also of how the carving hadn't matched what she'd started assuming was the girl's handwriting. "Maybe. It's certainly possible."

"So I've been doing some research on ghosts." Hayden peeled the back off the sticker and stuck it on the door upside-down. "Things about how to keep a ghost out of an area. And I read that if you turn your keyholes upside down, it confuses the dead and they can't get in. But, of course, we don't have keyholes, not anymore, and there's no way to turn the electronics upside down. Well, I mean, there probably is, but I don't know how. So I thought, hey, maybe I could get a pretend keyhole, and it would do the same thing." Hayden took a step back, admiring her handywork. "Maybe it'll be even more confusing, since it's not real. Though it does raise questions. Why does the alignment of a keyhole confuse a ghost? Do ghosts use keyholes to get into places? I can't imagine most doors actually have any sort of keyhole."

Martie placed her hand over the pendant and her heart, touched. "You didn't have to get that for me."

"Well, it is my room, too. I had that last pillow perfect on softness, and now I've got to start all over again." Hayden smiled.

Martie smiled back, but she couldn't hold it long. "I hope this works. I don't know how much more of this I can take." But she thought of the message on the chemistry bench—*giving up?*—and knew that she'd keep at it.

Chapter Eight

LUNCH WAS ALMOST over by the time Martie and Hayden made it back to the cafeteria. Hayden had spent the walk back trying to explain what exactly her family did, but all Martie had really been able to absorb was that Hayden's family had been going to Greyson Academy for generations, since the school was founded in the 1890s, and that they held a lot of power over the Board of Directors and the way the school functioned. Hayden's family probably could directly affect Ms. Molina's job. No wonder she'd backed off.

The cafeteria was half-empty, most kids having already wandered on to the next class. Martie hurriedly went through the line and took her food to one of the empty tables. Hayden plopped down beside her and dug in.

"It really wasn't fair of her to imply I was acting out because of how my life's been going lately," Martie said around a carrot stick. "That's a horrible thing to say to a kid who has just lost her parents."

"It really is," Hayden agreed. "Though it is probably true in some cases." She took another bite of her sandwich, chewing thoughtfully. "If you don't mind me asking, how did your parents die?"

Martie instinctively flinched away from the question, but she forced herself to consider it. It was a fair question and avoiding thinking of it wasn't helping anything. "It was a car accident. They were driving together down I-10 and were rear-ended by a semi. The car spun out and was hit by the semi again." Martie swallowed hard. "They said they died quickly."

Hayden winced. "I'm so sorry."

"What about you?" Martie looked up to find Sinclair sitting on the other end of the table, typing away on her laptop. Had she been there the whole time? Martie hadn't noticed, but she had been pretty focused on her food.

"What do you mean, 'what about me'?"

Sinclair gave her a weird look. "What happened to you?"

"What?"

"What happened to you during the accident?"

Martie blinked a few times, trying to decide if Sinclair was messing with her somehow. "I don't know what you mean. I wasn't there."

Sinclair brushed some hair behind one ear. "Where were you?"

"I was…" Martie trailed off. Where *had* she been? At home? At school? Nothing was coming, no memories of where she was when she'd learned of her parents' deaths, or what she'd been doing up to that point.

"Martie." Martie looked up to find Sinclair staring at her, her expression naked and open. "Martie, you were in the car with your parents."

Martie laughed, but it sounded feeble. "No, I wasn't. I would remember."

Sinclair watched her another moment, then turned her laptop around so Martie could see her screen. *Daughter Survives Deadly Crash Without a Scratch* read the headline, and the website had the logo for one of Tucson's local news channels.

Beside her, Hayden put her hands over her mouth.

"There is one light amidst all this darkness," Sinclair said, as if she were quoting something. "Martina Torsney, 16, who was in the backseat of her family's vehicle, was thrown clear of the crash and survived without any major injury."

"But—" Martie started, then stopped. She could...she could remember. She had been in the backseat, staring out the car window, not thinking about anything in particular. Then, a sickening crash, the back of the car ramming into her, and the slow motion as she found herself outside the car, flying toward the median. And then...nothing. Nothing, until she'd woken up again in the hospital, Aunt Jessica hovering anxiously over her bed.

Almost in a trance, Martie rolled up the sleeve on her left forearm. A long, angry scar graced it, the hints of stitches left in the edges. She could almost remember, now, how she'd been wearing long sleeves since the accident to cover it up.

"That's definitely a scratch," Hayden said.

Martie blinked, reconnecting with the world and finding her face wet. "How?" she asked. "How could I have forgotten?"

"It's not uncommon," said Sinclair, snapping her laptop shut. "Lots of people suppress traumatic memories."

Yeah, sure, she'd heard that before, but this was insane. How could she ever have forgotten that she was there when her parents died? Her brain had locked the entire thing up tight—no wonder she hadn't been able to focus on her parents' deaths at all.

Hayden frowned in Sinclair's direction. "Why are you looking up Martie's parents' deaths? That's an invasion of privacy."

Sinclair tossed her hair. "Really, Hayden? You didn't search Martie before she showed up?"

"I would never." Hayden sniffed.

"It is weird," Martie said, pleased to have something else to focus on, "that you were looking at that. Why were you?"

Sinclair shoved her laptop back into her bag and stood up. "Look, I am helping. Martie can't process something she doesn't even know happened, and now she knows, and she can deal with it." She pulled her bag on over her shoulder and stalked out of the cafeteria.

Martie stared down at her food, no longer interested in it. "Is there a nurse, or a counselor, on campus?"

Hayden nodded. "Do you want me to show you?"

"Yes, please."

What Martie really wanted was to go back to her room and cry into her pillow, or maybe even go home to Arizona and cry into her own pillow, in her own room. But she couldn't do that—she no longer had a room since her parents no longer had a house—and ditching classes right after Ms. Molina tried to put her on probation wasn't going to help anything, either.

A medical professional would give her an excuse, and it would give her time to think.

The school had both, which was not a surprise, in a different set of offices than the administrative ones but directly across from the others. Hayden explained what had happened and they let Martie into a darkened room to lie on a couch and be alone with her thoughts, though they did offer to have someone for her to talk to when she was ready.

No wonder everything had felt so disconnected and weird the last couple of months. Martie had chalked it up to grief, to not being able to process her parents' deaths because everything was too recent, too raw, but if she'd been suppressing what had actually happened, her brain must have been going through mental gymnastics to keep everything in the cage she'd made.

She peeled her sleeve back again, running her fingers down the scar there. It was raised and obvious, and she got a vague memory of it wrapped in bandages, blood seeping through, while at the hospital. Was that when she'd started suppressing everything? Maybe. Aunt Jessica had never pushed her about talking about the accident—they'd mutually and individually decided that it was too painful—so it had probably been fairly easy. No one ever knows what to say to someone who has just experienced tragedy, and it had been summer break anyway. She'd just hidden herself away in Aunt Jessica's house and buried everything.

Interesting, that all that deception had only taken one news article to break. But Hayden was right. Why the hell had Sinclair been looking up her parents' deaths? And why right now? Or had she looked it up ages ago, and had just kept it up to spring on Martie when the time felt right? What in the world was her goal with that?

How many people had looked up her parents' deaths and knew Martie had been in the accident too? It was natural curiosity, she supposed, and probably wouldn't be that hard to find. Ms. Molina probably knew, too. Whoever had sponsored her scholarship had probably included it.

That was no doubt why she'd gotten in. "This poor orphan was the only survivor of the car accident that killed both her parents. Her only living relative, that she knows of, is her aunt, who has five children of her own and a hard enough time handling all of them. Her grades are decent."

Could be worse, she supposed. She could have been sent off to some obscure relative in a castle somewhere, where she would have been harvested for her organs or whatever happened to people in those stories.

Not for the first time, she wondered what exactly her grandparents had done or said to have her parents cut them out of their lives.

Okay. Where did she go from here? She traced the scar again. Did this actually change anything? Her parents were still dead, she still had a scholarship here, and this was still her chance to make sure that she stayed strong, and kept herself together, and was successful. Not just for herself, but for her parents' memories.

"You have been touched by death." A quiet voice, so quiet Martie wasn't sure it wasn't just in her head. She raised herself up on her elbows and looked around the darkened room.

The girl was in the corner, about as far away from Martie as she could be in that room. She glowed, but barely, oddly clear even in the darkness. "You have been touched by death," the girl said again, though it still sounded like someone very far away. "That is why they brought you here. That is why I can see you."

"Why you can see me? Don't you mean, why I can see you?"

In response, the girl faded away.

The nurse stuck her head in. "Did you need something?"

"No, I'm fine." Martie stared at the corner.

That's why I can see you.

Chapter Nine

"HOW ARE YOU holding up?" Hayden sat her tray down next to Martie's spot at the table and placed some rolls in front of Martie.

Martie shrugged, staring down at the rolls. They smelled amazing, and her stomach rumbled mutinously.

She'd left the office after the ghost had gone, not wanting to stay in the darkened room anymore and think of what might be lurking in there. The girl had been as close as ever, even though Martie had still been wearing her pendant. Did that mean that the pendant wasn't working? That the girl had chosen not to appear again until that moment? Or did it mean that it took more work for her to appear?

Whatever the case was, lying in a dark room where she'd seen a ghost had not been appealing.

The nurse had made her set up a counseling appointment before she'd left. Martie couldn't imagine what good that was going to do, but whatever. And, then, since it'd been mid-afternoon, Martie had gone to her programming class and then to martial arts—whatever it was—before collapsing on her bed, which was where Hayden had found her and made her go to dinner.

Martie had thought of so many questions that she could have asked the ghost. What had the girl done to the previous scholarship students? Had she been the one to trash her and Hayden's room? What did the girl mean, that she could see Martie? Could she not see other people? Was, say, Hayden, invisible to the spirit world or whatever?

Not like the girl would have answered. And just remembering her voice made Martie's skin crawl.

She reached out and picked up one of the rolls. It was warm in her hand. "I saw the ghost again today."

Hayden went pale but, to her credit, did not turn away from Martie.

Martie started tearing the bread into pieces. "She said I'd been touched by death, and that's why she could see me."

"Why *she* could see *you*?"

"That's what I said!" Martie ran out of roll and picked up the other one. "Not like she answered. But I was thinking…" She took a deep breath, unsure if she actually wanted to say this out loud. It sounded crazy in her mind. "I was thinking that, if being touched by death means that ghosts can see me, maybe…" She took another breath, closing her eyes. "Maybe my parents can see me, too."

Hayden said nothing.

Martie opened her eyes to find Hayden watching her with wide, sad eyes. "Oh, Martie," she said.

"I know, I know." Tears streaked down her cheeks. She'd cried more today than she had since she was a kid.

Hayden laid a gentle hand on her arm. "I think it's good that you haven't seen your parents. They wouldn't be here, right? They'd be back home in Arizona, and you were there for a while before you came here. Not seeing them means that they've passed on. They're not trapped here; they don't have unfinished business. That's good. That's happy. They're at peace."

Martie dropped the remains of her roll and dug her palms into her eyes, though this did nothing to stop the flow of tears. Hayden was right—that was a good sign. She didn't want her parents to not be able to move on, but all the same… "I just miss them so much. How could they leave me?"

Hayden wrapped her arms around Martie, patting her head gently. "Shh. It's all right. They didn't want to leave you, I'm sure. But I'm also sure that wherever they are, they're watching you, and they're proud of you."

Martie's body shook. In the back of her mind, she was aware that they were in the dorm's cafeteria, and that there must be other people there, watching, and that it would be all over the dorm and probably the school that she'd had some sort of breakdown during dinner, but now that the tears were coming, they wouldn't stop. Had she cried for her parents before? Had she cried at all?

There'd been the funeral, of course. Martie had worn a long, black dress—with long sleeves—that had been too hot for the Arizona sun, even though they'd done the burial part pretty early in the morning. Everything had been closed casket. You can't say goodbye to a box, but understandably no one had wanted to see what had remained after the car accident. All she could recall feeling, as those boxes had been lowered into dirt, was a sense of being tired, yet feeling like she had to be strong, so that everyone would see how well she was dealing with this. How proud her parents would be of her.

Hayden held her for a long time. Finally, the tears subsided, though Martie was horrified to find she'd gotten snot all up Hayden's arm. She wiped her eyes and looked up to see what the social damage had been.

To her surprise, no one was looking at her and, on the table in front of her, was an array of plates. More rolls, a cupcake, some mashed potatoes. Mac and cheese, and a bowl of chicken noodle soup. A steaming mug of hot chocolate.

Tears stung the corners of her eyes again, but they didn't come. She probably didn't have anything left in her tear ducts.

Hayden patted her arm, smiling and seemingly unaware of the snot. "It's going to be okay."

Martie took the hot chocolate, savoring the warmth through her palms. "Do you think I can contact my parents? I mean, I agree, it's good that they're not haunting me, but I would like to say goodbye. And, you know, you hear stories about dead people answering phones or coming in the night."

Hayden's smile wavered a bit. "That's outside of my area of expertise. But I do know that you are not going to use a Ouija board for this, or anything that might make things worse and let something like that ghost girl in."

That was smart. Martie nodded slightly. She'd need to do more research or, ideally, find someone who knew what the hell they were doing. How she was going to do that when she was stuck on this hilltop in the middle of the forest in the middle of nowhere, Vermont, was beyond her, but the thought did make her feel a little better about the whole thing. If there was a safe way to do this, she would figure it out.

MARTIE SLEPT HEAVILY that night, too exhausted for even her dreams to haunt her, and woke up only when Hayden shook her. The overwhelming despair from the day before had lessened somewhat, though her heart still ached, and the beginnings of a headache were already starting to come on. She dressed hurriedly—slacks and a cardigan, since her skirts and sweaters were dirty—and headed down to breakfast. Food was still not exciting, but she forced herself to get and eat some bacon and two pancakes.

Sinclair was sitting across the cafeteria, her attention on Martie, eyes narrowed. Martie looked up and caught her eyes a few times, but Sinclair's expression never changed. Strange cookie, that one.

Hayden, however, was unnecessarily cheerful. She praised Martie's choice of food and each bite she ate, offered to get her more, and patted her shoulder at least seven times.

Which was worse, here? The overprotective, trying-too-hard friend, or the class bully watching you suspiciously? Despite the show of kindness the night before, Martie did regret doing her crying in public. People never knew how to deal with grieving. And Ms.

Molina's words—that she was unstable because of the upheaval in her life—stuck in her brain.

After breakfast, they headed to school. It was bitterly cold, the autumn colors having seemingly changed from vibrant to rotting overnight, and though Martie wore her coat and a hat, the chill still seeped inside her bones. She practically jogged the whole way in between buildings. Martie paused only once, when she glanced out across the landscape and saw the girl, standing in the graveyard and watching Martie pass. Martie's heart shuddered, but she forced herself to keep moving after a second.

Though, later, she wondered why she had not pointed the girl out to Hayden, to see if Hayden could see her as well.

The halls were louder than normal, and, as they approached their history classroom, they could see Ms. Molina, Mrs. Weissman, and some men that Martie did not recognize standing outside. The rest of their class was gathered around, but no one was going in. Martie and Hayden slowed, joining the group. "What's going on?" Hayden asked.

Noor shook her head. "Don't know. We can't go in, for some reason."

Mrs. Weissman and Ms. Molina had their heads bent together, whispering. After a few moments, Ms. Molina looked up, met Martie's eyes, and immediately soured. "Miss Torsney," she said, loud enough that her voice echoed down the corridor. "If you would come here, please."

Martie shared a confused glance with Hayden and pushed through the rest of the sophomores. "Yes, Ms. Molina?"

In response, Ms. Molina simply pulled open the classroom door and motioned for Martie to step inside.

The class quieted around her as Martie stepped past Ms. Molina and into chaos.

It was her and Hayden's room all over again. Papers scattered everywhere, the stuffing inside the chair cushions pulled out, scratches in the whiteboard. And, everywhere, on every wall, on the side of Mrs. Weissman's desk, in the middle of the table, was carved, "Martie was here."

"What the hell?" Martie ran her fingers down one of the carvings. It was deep, rough, like it been done with, oh, a pair of scissors, maybe. Felt real, and obviously hadn't faded, not if there had been time to get Ms. Molina and those men. Security guards, maybe?

"I was hoping you could tell me." Ms. Molina had gone completely to ice, no trace of her fake smile or customer service tone of voice left. "I thought I was clear the other morning."

Martie's heart sank. Ms. Molina still thought she was doing this. "You were, yes."

"Then what, pray tell, is all this?" Ms. Molina gestured to the room at large.

"I'll tell you what it is." Hayden pushed her way into the room, and half the class followed her. "Someone is trying to get Martie expelled. And that someone is not Martie."

"Miss Lambert, if you would—"

"No, I agree." Mrs. Weissman, too, came into the room. She put her hands on her ample waist and surveyed the damage, frowning especially at her desk. "What is the point?"

"The point?" Ms. Molina stuttered. "Look, what we have here is a blatant disregard for school property, and it must be dealt with."

"You're telling me that Miss Torsney," Mrs. Weissman glanced at Martie, then away, "snuck into the school building in the middle of the night, broke into my classroom, did massive amounts of damage, and then simply went back to her room to go through her morning routine? It does not seem possible."

Wow. Martie wasn't sure whether to be insulted or grateful.

Ms. Molina glowered at the history teacher. "This is not a discussion to have here. Miss Torsney will need to come with me."

"She will not." Mrs. Weissman spun her desk chair around and sank into it, a few clouds of stuffing floating into the air. "If you will take your seats, students, we will begin our new unit."

What in the world? Martie tentatively set her bag down next to her normal seat. After a moment, Hayden crossed to her seat, and then Noor, and, slowly, the rest of the class. Ms. Molina watched them, her face turning an impressive shade of purple.

"Now, then," Mrs. Weissman said, pushing herself back to her feet. Ignoring the carving in the whiteboard, she wrote, "Themes in cultural stories."

"Mrs. Weissman," Ms. Molina hissed. "This is not acceptable."

Mrs. Weissman gave her a look that Martie had seen aimed at her fellow students—and herself—more than once. "Where is your proof, Ms. Molina? My lock was not broken, so whoever did this must have had a key to my room. Or they came in through my unbroken, locked windows. Just because a child's name is written on the wall does not mean that said child did the deed. In fact, general logic would state that, in most cases, a perpetrator would not want to take credit for something like this. Like I tell my students, back up your statement with proof, or do not disrupt class."

Ms. Molina sputtered, then turned on her heel and left, though her heels did not echo on the carpet. They did outside, in the hallway, and they could hear her stomp all the way down to the office.

"Now, then," Mrs. Weissman said. "Stories are as important to a culture as their form of government, or how they treat their people. What kinds of stories are told tell you a significant amount about what is important and how a culture thinks. That being said, some themes we see repeated through cultures across the world and across different time periods."

This was surreal. The "Martie was here" in the table was within her reach from where she sat, and there was a definite hole in her chair where the stuffing had been torn out. Half of the other kids were stealing glances at her, but the others were focused on Mrs. Weissman, like this was all normal.

Martie couldn't believe Ms. Molina—or those men—hadn't dragged her to the front door and thrown her out. She pinched herself on the arm, just in case.

Mrs. Weissman was making a list of themes on the board, right over the scratches. It was an odd mix of things: jealousy, human shapeshifters, underwater civilizations, great floods, evil forests, not belonging.

Martie pulled her notebook out of her bag and started copying the list down.

"Now," Mrs. Weissman continued, "there are some people who believe, especially in folklore themes that are found the world over, that there must be some element of truth to those stories. How do civilizations across the world come up with the idea of an underwater civilization if there is not and has never been any evidence toward that being true? Well, you must consider—"

The door to the classroom slammed open. Martie jumped.

Mr. Brooks rushed in. "No! You must be lenient! You must..." He trailed off, staring at the gathered class in confusion. "I'm sorry, I'd heard that there'd been a..." He frowned at the walls. "...an incident."

Mrs. Weissman pinched the bridge of her nose. "Mr. Brooks, I have had quite enough interruptions for this morning. Do you not have a class of your own for this period?"

Mr. Brooks' eyes fell on Martie. He scanned the room again, then looked back at her, confusion written across his features. "I apologize, Mrs. Weissman. Apparently, I have...misunderstood the situation." He left, glancing around the entire way out.

Mrs. Weissman sighed heavily. "Now, where was I? Oh, yes. Let us consider, for example, the evil forest theme. You see this in Europe in the fairy tale form of story, where the forest is a place where witches and wolves lurk, waiting to eat people. You see it in South America, where portions of the forest are so evil even the animals will not enter them. And you see it here, in the native stories. According to local stories, though I will say that the native peoples of this area were driven out many years ago, and the stories that have been passed down may have experienced some drift, there is a section of forest, not far from here, that was considered evil by the people and the animals. Now, what might cause these stories? It is hard to say. In many cases, such as the one here, they say there is a creature of some sort that lurks within. In reality, this is probably a bear, or a wolf, of some sort, that someone saw once, and the story has been exaggerated since then."

She pointed to the board. "Your assignment, for this week, is to choose one of these themes, or another one that you can prove exists in at least four different cultures, preferably on different continents, and to find stories that fit it. Then we shall compare and contrast the elements of the story and see if we can guess what the basis behind the story theme is."

Martie waited, but apparently Mrs. Weissman was done. Around her, everyone began to pull out their laptops. Martie did the same, catching sight of some more chair stuffing scattered across the floor underneath the table. This was insane. How was everyone just going about their day like this was normal? Martie opened her laptop, staring at the list of themes.

"Which are you going to do?" Noor whispered to her.

"Not evil forests, I can tell you that. We barely have trees in Arizona, so I'm already weirded out by them as it is."

Noor laughed. "I'm going to do human shapeshifters, I think. Or maybe something about monsters that look human except for a single attribute that gives them away."

"Oof, that's scary."

"I know, isn't it great?"

Martie returned to staring at the list. Yeah, definitely not forests. The last thing she needed right now was to think about what was out there that the ghost wanted to lead her to. Not belonging was perhaps too obvious, and she didn't need to be pointing out to anyone how she was different, not right now, not with someone trying to get her thrown out.

That had to be it, right? Martie focused on the carving in the table. It was the same handwriting as the carving in her and Hayden's room. But not the ghost's handwriting. Or maybe it was, and there was a different mechanism between phantom writing that faded away and actual damage.

But no, it was more likely that someone was trying to get her kicked out, and the worse thing was that Ms. Molina was totally falling for it. A chill traveled down her spine. Who could hate her so much to do all this and pin it on her? She'd only been at school a few weeks, and she couldn't remember any interactions that were especially heated, aside from some with Sinclair. Martie peeked at her, across the table, like always. She had her hair back in a tight bun, typing away at lightspeed. She was not paying Martie any mind.

If Sinclair had it out for Martie, she was doing a fantastic job of hiding it.

Which went back to the whole scholarship student angle. Seriously, if the school had lost all, uh, fifteen or whatever of its scholarship students, you'd think they'd learn to check in on them more or something the next time they tried. Do something to protect them from the rest of the student body, if bullying was an issue, especially to this level.

Right, she needed to pick a topic.

Ms. Molina didn't return during history, and neither did Martie see her during trig. The story had spread impressively, though, considering that they'd all been together, and half the same people went to trig. All the new people had already heard, and people kept turning around in class to stare at her.

She did her best to focus, but it was hard. Where was Ms. Molina? Was she putting together the expulsion papers while Martie sat here and learned her trig identities? Were they packing up Martie's room and arranging for her to fly back to Arizona?

Well, that was one thing, she guessed. If she got sent back to Arizona, she wasn't going to end up in the woods with the ghost. Instead, she'd have the ghost of what she'd lost.

She made it to chemistry without incident. Mr. Brooks was there, of course, and he smiled wildly at Martie as she arrived. Martie smiled back, but she felt jittery, disconnected, and it had been weird that Mr. Brooks had heard about the incident down in Mrs. Weissman's class so quickly and had rushed to her defense. She knew he wanted to help her feel comfortable at the school, but something about the whole thing felt…performative.

She was reading too much into it.

Martie slid into her desk, where'd they sit until it was time to start their experiments, if they were doing one. Reaching into her bag, she pulled out the notebook she was using for notes.

A slip of paper floated to the floor.

Huh. Martie didn't remember putting that in there or doing anything that would have ripped off a piece. She picked it up, flipping it over.

They won't kick you out. The scholarship students are needed.

Martie recognized the handwriting—it matched the note that had come with her pendant, and was definitely different than both the "GET OUT" messages and "Martie was here" carvings. She peeked up at Mr. Brooks, but he'd moved his attention to something on his desk.

Scholarship students were needed? Needed for what?

To fulfill a quota, probably. Something token, to get grant money or state funding or who knew what.

But, still, everything seemed to come back to the scholarship thing. She needed more information. Not like Ms. Molina was going to give it to her, though, not now, and she'd been cagey about it before anyway. And the archives were a bust, unless there were other folders like the one she'd already found, or unless she got some dates.

Wait, she had some dates. There had been years on those photos she'd found. She could look through the appropriate materials and see if there was more on those specific students.

Great. A way forward.

Chapter Ten

ON HER WAY out of chemistry, Mr. Brooks stopped her. "I don't want you to worry, Martina. I'm going to make sure you're not prosecuted for something you didn't do."

What a strange statement. If he'd left the note in her bag, he wouldn't need to follow it up verbally.

But if he hadn't left the note in her bag... And he probably hadn't. When would he have put it in? She didn't remember it in math, which meant someone must have slipped it in at the very end of that period, or perhaps passing in the hall. Which meant that the pendant had also not been from Mr. Brooks.

Martie stared at him, a sinking feeling in her stomach, though it was not his fault that he had not helped her as she had assumed he had. "How do you know I didn't do it?" she asked.

The eternal smile on Mr. Brooks' face faltered. "What do you mean? Did you do it?"

"No, of course not. But you seem...very sure."

The smile was back. "I am an excellent judge of character, Martina. You are a serious person, and I know you wouldn't throw away an opportunity like this." He continued on, but Martie stopped paying attention. Why *was* he so sure? Well, it didn't matter. She needed to go, or she wasn't going to get a chance to get to the archives before lunch was over.

"I appreciate your confidence in me," Martie finally broke in, using her best teacher smile. "Thank you for your help in trying to clear my name."

Mr. Brooks nodded and opened his mouth to say more, but Martie booked it for the door, clinging to the strap of her bag. It wasn't like her to run from a teacher, but hopefully he'd chalk it up to stress or something.

Everything came back to the scholarship. She needed to figure out what was happening with that.

Hayden was gone, but maybe this would be all right. Taking a deep breath, Martie ran down the main staircase to the second floor. The library was fairly empty, and the librarian was not at her desk. Oh well. It wasn't like the woman knew the archives any better than Martie did. She slowed as she approached the door, which was open. Somehow, that felt like a violation, though the archives were open to anybody. After a moment, the door opened wider, and Sinclair stepped out, almost immediately locking eyes with Martie.

Martie froze but forced herself to move after a moment. This was fine. Sinclair could do whatever she wanted, and it wasn't like Martie was doing anything wrong.

Sinclair sniffed as Martie passed. "You might want to be careful," she said, her voice barely carrying. "You don't want your…unhelpful friend to follow you in here. The stuff in the archives is one of a kind and can't be replaced." She tossed her hair and disappeared into the stacks.

Martie's unhelpful friend? The ghost? No. Sinclair obviously didn't know about the ghost, not with her mocking from earlier. She probably meant whoever was carving Martie's name all over the school. So, was that an admission of guilt? Or confirmation that Sinclair didn't believe Martie was doing it herself?

It didn't matter. Martie needed to find out more about the scholarship students. She pushed the door to the archives back open. Let's see…there'd been George in 1916, and Alice in 1943, and Donna…

A file lay in the middle of the floor.

God, the ghost was anticipating her now. Martie knelt and flipped it open. Inside was a single sheet of paper, handwritten, similar to the pendant/note handwriting but not the same. Older, by the yellowing along the edges of the paper.

List of scholarship students at Greyson Academy, it said across the top. And then, below, was a list of names, each accompanied by a year. George Miller, 1916, was not the first. The first was Donald Cooper, 1891, just shortly after the school opened. But, yes, as she'd been told, there was a ten to twenty-year gap between each scholarship student.

This was a goldmine. Judging by the years, this was everybody. Every scholarship student, and years for all, which meant she could look up more information about each one. Or, hell, maybe she could search them on the Internet. That'd worked all right for the others, and she wouldn't even need to dig through the archives.

On the very bottom of the list, in different handwriting—the pendant/note handwriting—someone had added Martie's name, and "TBD" instead of a year, written in pencil, where the rest was pen.

Every hair on Martie's skin stood up. TBD—to be determined—for what? To be determined when she, too, would leave the school?

No. She didn't know that something had happened to every one of these people. No reason to jump to horrible, horrible conclusions.

Okay. 1891. Martie tucked the folder and its list into her bag, digging around in a couple of boxes until she figured out what organization existed. It was mostly by year, as the librarian had said, with the oldest boxes being to the left of the door. The years increased in a clockwise circle from there, with the newest being off to the right. The oldest boxes didn't have much—some photos, some articles, the occasional letter. Nothing about Donald Cooper, but maybe everything had been lost over the years. Martie moved on to George Miller, but though the 1916 box had more stuff in it, there was no note of George Miller at all. No articles about his disappearance. No photos, though there was one of a group of three boys in which only two were named.

Martie ignored the goosebumps rising on her arms. This was explainable. Maybe everything about George had been in that other folder. Maybe whoever had put that one together had taken everything they could about him. So it made sense that nothing was left here in 1916. She should check someone else, someone not in the other folder.

Consulting the list, Martie noted that the person before her, about twelve years ago, was a boy named Justin Costa. Martie slid 1916 back into place and headed to the appropriate part of the room. More recent years had fewer boxes again, probably because so much had moved online. Martie chose one at random and starting leafing through it. It was a good thing there weren't that many students at any one time, or this would be impossible.

This box had photographs again. Candid shots, selfies, a few that were verging on inappropriate, most of which had obviously been printed out, and not very well. Martie flipped several over but didn't see Justin's name on any of them. There were letters too, and printed-out emails. A couple of reports. A mess, really. Who decided what got saved?

Nothing from Justin. None of his reports, no pictures of his smiling face. Martie put the box back and grabbed another one and, when that one also yielded nothing, another. This one was class pictures, not unlike the one Martie had been given her first day, as well as other more formal portraits. Taking out the four class pictures, Martie laid them out in order.

Justin wasn't on any of them.

Martie twisted some hair around a finger. Where was he? For a wild second, she considered the possibility that all the scholarship students had been fabricated, made up to fulfill some quota, and whoever had approved Martie's enrollment hadn't gotten the memo. But, no, that made even less sense. If you'd made someone up, you'd leave evidence of them.

The junior class picture had a blank spot. Unlike on Martie's, there was no note of a future student coming soon. The other classes were full. Martie moved them to the side, picking up the junior year picture. On hers, each student's name was under their picture, but on this one, the names were printed in black ink on the photos themselves, which made some of them difficult to read. Also, compared to the other class pictures, this one was oddly stiff. Martie wobbled it up and down a few times, then picked up the sophomore one and did the same. Yeah, definitely different. Martie moved it closer to her face. It was shinier too, like someone had put a layer of veneer on the top, whatever sense that made. Gently, with a single fingernail, she scratched over the blank picture spot, but nothing came up.

Frowning, Martie twisted the picture around again, holding it up so it reflected the light. It was almost like it was laminated. She ran her fingernails along the sides, and, on the bottom, the layers separated.

A odd sense of triumph—from potentially destroying pictures?—ran through her. As carefully as she could, she pulled the top layer off the rest. It came fairly easily, and was, for the most part, transparent, exactly like it had been laminated.

Except, over the blank picture, there was a dark oval, just the size of one of the other pictures. And underneath it…underneath it was Justin Costa. He had a good jawline and a winning smile, and freckles across his nose, just like she did, though there was no further resemblance, as he was dirty blond and had a bit of a sunburn across his nose and cheeks.

This...this had been deliberate. The age of the materials couldn't be an excuse here. Someone had come in and covered Justin up, like he had never existed.

Like none of them had existed.

Martie stuffed that picture in her bag too, inside the folder. She needed...she needed to talk to someone. She needed answers.

On a hunch, she crossed to the newest boxes, from just the year before. Hayden had said her original roommate hadn't returned. Maybe the school didn't like people who didn't finish. Maybe anyone who left would be erased from the archives. If that was true, she'd find another blank spot where Hayden's roommate had been the year before.

She dug through the boxes until she found the class pictures again and pulled out the freshman one. Familiar faces stared back at her. Except for one. A Lindsay Muneca. But she was still there, still smiling.

No one had erased her.

The folder in Martie's bag seemed impossibly heavy.

Chapter Eleven

THE NEXT DAY saw more of a return to normalcy. Ms. Molina never reappeared, either to throw Martie out of the school or to apologize, and the other kids in her classes were mostly over the whole thing. Sure, some kids were coming straight from a class in Mrs. Weissman's classroom, but even they seemed to be over the whole thing fairly quickly. Maybe, since Martie's room had been vandalized much the same way, all the conversations and arguments on the subject had been had, and there was nothing really left to say.

But, still, the folder weighed heavy in her bag. She should talk to someone. Who? Hayden, maybe. She didn't necessarily know anything about the scholarship students, but her family had connections with the school, so maybe she could find things out. If nothing else, she would be a sympathetic ear. But, still—was she putting too much on Hayden? Martie'd only known her for less than a month, and Hayden had already put up with more than any roommate realistically should. And she'd gone out of her way to get that keyhole sticker for Martie too.

Well, Martie would leave her as an option.

There was Mr. Brooks. He knew something about the previous scholarship students, and he'd offered to help. He was an option, too, but it felt weird to bring it up with a teacher. Still, he probably had access to materials that Martie, and other students, wouldn't.

And there was Sinclair. What did the other girl know?

Sinclair already thought she was batty. She should probably burn that bridge first, even if it eternally ruined her social life here at Greyson.

Because, she suspected, if she didn't figure out what was going on with the scholarship students soon, her social life wouldn't have a chance to matter.

After school, Martie trudged down the path toward the dorm. There was martial arts today. If Martie was quick, she could catch Sinclair after class. Like the other kids, she'd taken to wearing her gi so she could just shed her coat and shoes and go straight into class. In theory, she could just put them back on, but Sinclair was lightning fast and always long gone before Martie was ready, or she went into the locker room, and Martie wasn't going back in there if she could help it.

Hayden wasn't in the room, which was just as well. Martie set her bag next to her chair and changed. She had a few minutes before she needed to head out, so now was as good a time as any. Sitting on the floor in the middle of the room, she closed her eyes and took several deep breaths.

Though Hayden had made several good points as to why she shouldn't do this, Martie couldn't help but think that there had to be some way to reach her parents one last time. Just to say goodbye. If ghosts were real, why shouldn't she be able to?

So she took several slow, deep breaths, focusing on them, clearing her mind as best she could. Then she pictured her parents in her mind, their smiling faces, the way her dad almost always had a pencil behind his ear, and the way her mother would let her hair down the instant she got home from work, to symbolically break its hold over her life. She pictured them reaching out to her and reached back for them, willing them into existence.

But they were just images. And no matter how much Martie pictured them, hoped for them, wanted them, they never became anything else. There was never a feeling of love, of peace, like people in stories talked about.

There was just emptiness.

Martie opened her eyes, wiping at her cheeks, and found the ghost floating in front of her.

She looked the same as always, but Martie got the feeling that she was curious more than anything.

"Why can I see you but not them?" Martie asked. "Why won't they say goodbye?"

The ghost cocked her head to one side but said nothing. She faded from view, a half-hearted *get out* following her to wherever she went.

Great. So helpful.

Wiping her cheeks more, Martie pushed to her feet. Outside, she could hear another door shutting. Sinclair's, maybe? Oh! If Martie could catch her on the way there, then she wouldn't need to worry about trying to do so after. She hurriedly grabbed her coat and water bottle and ran out. No sign of Sinclair on the stairs or in the atrium, but once Martie was outside, she could see Sinclair maybe fifty feet ahead, moving with her characteristic speed.

Come to me.

Martie slowed. They weren't words, not really, more of a whisper on the wind, and a definite tug toward the woods.

Come to me.

Okay, this was new and weird. Her ghost, trying once again to lure her somewhere?

But no, it didn't feel the same. And ghosts weren't supposed to learn new tricks.

Come to me.

Oh, for the love of God, Martie did not have time for this madness. She broke into a sprint. "Sinclair! Wait up!"

For several moments, Sinclair didn't react, but she did eventually slow down so that Martie could catch up. "What?" she said grumpily as Martie tried to catch her breath. "We're going to be late if we take too long."

"I wanted to ask you about something you said." Martie had to stop and take a couple more breaths. Maybe she needed to work out more. Or maybe it was the godforsaken cold. Why was it so cold? Why was anywhere so cold? And it wasn't even winter yet. "My first day, you said—"

Come to me!

Martie stumbled and almost fell off the side of the path.

Sinclair frowned at her. "Are you drunk?"

The pull from the woods was strong. It took real effort to keep herself on the path. Sinclair had actually stopped and was watching her closely, an unreadable expression on her face.

"Maybe we'd better just get to class," Martie said.

Sinclair nodded and Martie did her best to stay right next to her. What in the everloving world was this? She'd known the trees were potentially evil, but this was different, and way more direct, than she'd been picturing.

As they neared the rec center, the pull lessened completely, leaving Martie confused and out of breath. Sinclair led the way into class, and then there was no opportunity for conversation.

Martie let her mind wander as they moved through the positions. Walking to and from martial arts was her best chance to get Sinclair alone. In class or in the cafeteria, there would be other ears listening, and Martie was well aware that people already thought she was crazy and/or a destructive maniac. In theory, talking about scholarship students was understandable and normal, but there was something weird about the whole thing. Should she do more research on the computer first before talking to Sinclair?

Well, the way things were going, it wouldn't matter. As class closed and everyone began packing up, dread crept into Martie's stomach. She hurried so she could walk with Sinclair, who maybe even waited for her, and held her breath as she stepped outside.

Nothing. No pull. No words.

Still, Martie didn't relax until the dorm was in sight. "You said something about none of the scholarship students lasting," she said to Sinclair, who'd been focused on her phone the entire walk.

Sinclair blinked, as if she hadn't realized Martie was there. "So?"

"So, why not? What happened to them?"

Sinclair shrugged, her attention going back to her phone. "I don't know. Lots of things, I imagine."

This conversation was going nowhere. Martie resisted the urge to sigh. "Did someone…do something to them?"

Sinclair slid to a stop. "What? Why would you think that?"

Oh, so many reasons. The erasure from the archives, the ghost, this list with the dates—which someone was obviously tracking—this new pull from the woods, the fact no one would talk clearly about any of the other scholarship students. But if Sinclair didn't actually know anything… "It's weird, isn't it? That not a single one made it to graduation? Out of over 100 years of trying? What are the odds?"

Sinclair huffed. "I don't know, Martie. Things happen." She paused for half a second, then flipped her hair over her shoulder. "Poor people and rich people are different. Maybe as time went on, they realized that, and they felt like their future was elsewhere."

Ugh. Hearing that sort of opinion shouldn't have felt like a surprise—she'd come into this school dreading that sort of thinking—but it hurt, all the same. "Every single one of them?"

"That's how the world works. You should get used to it." Sinclair pushed past Martie.

Martie watched her go for a moment, trying to ignore the sinking feeling in her stomach. She'd started to think maybe she and Sinclair were getting along, to some extent, but apparently she was just kidding herself.

After a long moment, she followed after Sinclair. It was too dark and too cold to stay out here alone.

Hayden was in their room when Martie arrived, her head bent over her laptop as she worked on homework or something. Martie took a moment to change into comfortable clothes—old joggers and a sweatshirt—before taking out the folder from the archives and laying it open on her desk. Skipping the three she'd looked at already—George, Alice, and Donna—Martie ran searches on the others. The more recent ones were harder because there were tons of results for each name, and Martie didn't know where they'd come from before Greyson, so she had to add a "Greyson Academy" modifier to the search.

The results were, well, not promising. In some cases, like Donna, she could tell where they'd come from and when they'd been born, but in many cases, all she found was an article, noting that local teen so-and-so had received a scholarship to Greyson, and then nothing else. Even if Martie could figure out identifying characteristics, every single one of them had nothing— nothing at all, not even an obituary—after their time at Greyson.

They weren't just disappearing from the school— they were disappearing from everywhere.

Remembering Hayden's old roommate, Lindsay, Martie ran a search on her as well. Results popped up immediately. Apparently after she'd left, she'd gone to a different, prestigious school closer to home, and she had social media feeds that she updated fairly regularly with typical teen stuff. Well, rich teen stuff. The feeds started about the time that she left the school, since Greyson strongly discouraged wasting time on those sorts of activities. The first few posts sounded grumpy, like her leaving Greyson hadn't necessarily been her own choice, but she was definitely still out there.

So what had happened to the other scholarship students?

MARTIE BARELY resisted clutching Hayden's arm as they stepped out of the dorm the next morning into the chill, gray autumn. But, again, there was nothing. Martie darted a look toward the trees, but it was quiet and still, aside from the other students hurrying through the cold themselves. Had she imagined it all? Some sort of mental block to stop her from talking to Sinclair? What sense did that make?

Mrs. Weissman's room had been cleaned up in the two days since the vandalism. The scratches were still in the table and desk, but the chairs had been repaired, or replaced, and everything else had been put back.

Martie even saw Ms. Molina out in the hall, who gave her a cold smile and said nothing.

Mr. Brooks was really Martie's last chance. She could barely focus on math and chemistry. Hayden did the lab yet again—why did she keep pairing with Martie, seriously?—while Martie tried to inconspicuously watch the teacher and imagine how the conversation would go. He'd been cagey before, but maybe if she just laid out that she knew something had happened, he would come clean. What other choice did she have?

Finally, class ended. Martie sent Hayden on without her, promising to actually show up for lunch today. It took a few minutes for everyone else to trickle out.

Before she could lose her nerve, Martie marched up to the desk. "I know something bad happened to the other scholarship students."

Mr. Brooks startled, knocking a stack of papers onto the floor. Instead of cleaning them up, he stared at her, the same, confused look he'd given her so many times lately. "I beg your pardon?"

"I know that they all came here, and then they just…vanished." Martie threw her hands up, as if to symbolize their sudden non-existence. "No one was ever heard from again. I want to know what really happened to them."

"Martina, we've talked about this. People leave for different reasons."

"But they didn't leave. They disappeared. And the school tried to erase them."

"Erase them? Why would anyone do that?"

Why *would* anyone want to do that? Martie faltered, thrown off. "Something terrible must have happened. Something the school doesn't want anyone to know about."

Mr. Brooks shook his head. "Martina, I understand you've been having difficult times. But there's no conspiracy here." He stood, guiding her toward the door. "No one is out to get you. You're safe, and we are here to support you, and we'll get to the bottom of whatever is going on with the vandalism targeting you." He pushed her out into the hall and shut the door behind her.

Martie stood there, blinking. Behind the closed door, she heard Mr. Brooks start talking, maybe into the phone. She couldn't make out much, just words like "troubled," "not adjusting," and "concerned."

Great. She was going to have to talk to the counselor even more.

Down in the cafeteria, Hayden stirred her soup more than was necessary. "It just doesn't make any sense, Martie. If something happened to them while they were here at school, there would be some sort of trail. You don't disappear twenty people or whatever and have it not be noticed. People would get suspicious. People's families would come looking for them."

People's families would come looking for them.

They absolutely would. So, what, the school told them they'd gone somewhere else? Even so, the school would be the common factor, and people would get suspicious after a while. Inquiries would be made.

Maybe that was why the scholarship students were so spread out. So that people *wouldn't* remember. Generational amnesia or something.

Still, some families, like Hayden's, had been coming forever. Wouldn't they notice? Maybe that's what Sinclair had meant. Maybe her family had noticed that the scholarship students never finished, but never associated anything else with it.

After all, there was no reason to be concerned with charity cases.

All right, time for a subject change. "I read about a new way to contact the dead." Hayden frowned at her. "No seances or Ouija boards still, I swear. It's more, like, you take something that was important to the person and try to use it to reach out to them."

"Oh, Martie. I wish you would stop." Hayden sighed. "Did you bring anything that was more important to your parents than you? If anything would have a connection, wouldn't it be you?"

Wouldn't it be you? Martie's heart ached. "I guess not, because that hasn't worked."

"It hasn't worked because they're gone." Hayden reached over, laying a hand on Martie's arm. "I know this is hard. I wish I knew how to make it better."

"But, if ghosts are real—"

"Are they?" Hayden glanced around, then leaned in closer. "Martie, have you ever considered that what you've been seeing *hasn't* been a ghost?"

Martie pictured her, floating within reach, just the day before. No need to tell Hayden that her keyhole sticker hadn't worked. "What else would she be?"

"Well," Hayden started, fidgeting, "you have been under a lot of stress, with your parents dying and moving here and everything."

"You think I'm hallucinating?" Martie's voice was louder than she meant it to be, and a few people turned their heads in her direction.

"I don't know. I mean, no one else has seen this girl."

Somewhere, deep inside, fear curled around Martie's gut. It could be a possibility—hadn't she entertained it herself? But there'd been her clothes thrown about, and that door that had locked and unlocked itself…she hadn't done that herself.

"She's not a hallucination," she said, trying to sound surer than she was.

"Okay," Hayden gave in easily. "Then what if she's something else? A darker entity of some sort?" She leaned in even closer, her nose practically in Martie's ear. "I read that sometimes demons manifest as children, to lure in victims."

A demon? It could be possible, she guessed. Maybe that's why the girl had no eyes, only shadows where they should be. Wasn't that a characteristic of darker entities too? That they looked human, except for one thing that was wrong. Backwards feet, or mouths in their necks, or something like that.

And if the girl was trying to scare her off, or lead her into the forest, then the demon theory looked even better.

"What do I do if she is a demon?"

Hayden returned to her soup. "I don't know. Call a priest or something."

"Isn't that just for exorcisms?"

Hayden shrugged, and Martie let the matter drop so Hayden's soup could stop being neglected before lunch was over.

Martie did her best to focus on the rest of her school day, but it was hard when everything pointed to her being next in a long line of disappearances. And she'd gotten nowhere on figuring out what was happening, or why they'd disappeared. And what did the ghost have to do with anything? Or demon, or hallucination, or whatever it was supposed to be?

She was going to have a mental breakdown. That was going to be what they said about her when she disappeared.

Should she...just leave? Call Aunt Jessica and ask to be picked up? It would be giving up, and she hated to do that, especially when she had nothing to look forward to at home—and not even really home, just an echo of it. But would being miserable in Arizona be better than dealing with whatever was going on here?

The awful thing was that she wasn't sure.

Chapter Twelve

October

A WEEK PASSED without her disappearing into wherever, and without her seeing the ghost or hearing commands in her head. She wanted to let her guard down, to think that maybe things would calm down, go back to normal, but Martie still had that list of names and years on her desk, speaking to other kids who had probably thought just what she wanted to think. And even if this was a lull, it obviously was not nothing.

Besides, there were still the "Martie was here" carvings in Mrs. Weissman's room. Martie's guess was that they were harder to repair than her room had been, since someone had scratched them into the school's old wood paneling, whereas her room was plaster and paint for the most part. Mrs. Weissman continued to give them no mind, and the rest of her class seemed to be following her lead.

Would the vandal, whether it was a person or otherwise, try the same thing a third time, somewhere else? Or had they decided it was a lost cause, since Martie still sat here, in theory unfazed, and even the staff didn't seem to care?

And how did the vandalism tie into the disappearances? Did it?

The whole thing made Martie's head hurt, and she hadn't been sleeping well. Sometimes she woke up, convinced that she had heard something, only to find everything as it should have been, with Hayden snoring gently in her own bed. One night, she had watched Hayden sleep for several minutes, feeling irrationally jealous.

"Now, remember," Mrs. Weissman said in her heavy Texan accent, "we'll present our findings for discussion tomorrow in class. So please finish up your arguments and be prepared to share them with your classmates."

Martie frowned at her laptop. She'd gone with underwater civilizations in the end. They didn't have water in Arizona any more than they had trees, but there also wasn't any water immediately around the school that might be trying to kill her. Though she was staying away from the pool, just in case. Besides, she'd looked at shapeshifters for a bit, and that seemed to be based in othering as much as the not belonging theme.

She'd divided her research into three categories: civilizations that existed underwater, civilizations that had existed which were now underwater, and cities that had been found underwater. The existence of the last seemed like it could lead credence to the second category, though she'd had less luck finding facts that might back up a civilization of people actually living under the sea. Not that she believed such things existed, but there had to be a reason it was a theme in folklore, especially in Europe.

Though they'd never discussed people's choices in class, she had a general idea of what people had chosen though general gossip, and there was at least one other person doing the same topic. She hoped the additional classifications would give her an edge.

Noor, beside her, was humming under her breath as she typed. She had pages and pages of specters and entities that were mostly human, many accompanied by artwork. She would probably be able to talk for a whole class period. But, excepting Noor, most people weren't typing at all, not anymore. Mrs. Weissman firmly believed that the presentation of information and the ability to justify it was as important as the information itself.

Across the table, Sinclair stared at Martie over the top of her laptop. She held Martie's glance for a long moment before going back to her screen. Weird. Martie never knew what was going on in that girl's head.

Okay. She'd present her categories in order. They built off each other, after all. The civilization actively living underwater was the purest form of the myth, and the civilization that had existed and then sank combined that with potential history. And, of course, the cities that had been found underwater spoke for themselves. She had categories there, too—ones that had been identified through historical texts, and ones that—

Ms. Molina opened the door and stepped into the room.

Martie's heart immediately lurched, but without so much as a glance in her direction, Ms. Molina made her way around the table and entered a whispered conversation with Mrs. Weissman. It went on for several minutes. Martie tried half-heartedly to drag her attention back to her work—this wasn't about her; not everything was about her—but it didn't work, and several other people seemed to have also lost their focus.

Finally, Ms. Molina left. Martie stared at the closed door, picturing her clicking her way down the hallway in her heels. Not about her. Ms. Molina was in charge of many things here at school, and she hadn't said anything to Martie since the morning that Mrs. Weissman's classroom had been vandalized.

It took a while, but Martie did manage to regain her focus.

Class ended—still no bells, or anything that marked the end of class, but Martie just picked someone at the beginning of each period and started cleaning up when they did. Her presentation was in pretty good shape, if she did say so herself. Certainly, she felt more in control than she had with the Roman Empire/Han Dynasty mess. She'd just drop by her locker and grab her textbooks in case she needed them for the next few classes. There was a quiz in trigonometry, and sometimes they could use the book to look up identities.

The lockers were all together on the first floor, just outside the history classrooms. There didn't seem to be any organization to them—not one section for seniors, one for juniors, et cetera. Martie's was across the hall and halfway down from Hayden's. She ran through her combo a few times in her head. It would be second nature by some point, no doubt, but not yet.

She approached her locker and stopped dead in her tracks.

Someone—the same someone who was carving "Martie was here" everywhere—had, with marker, written "I want to die" in large capital letters on her locker. And, to top it off, they'd drawn a crude stick figure underneath with x's for eyes and their tongue sticking out.

Hot tears welled in the corners of her eyes. What was this person's problem?

Noor came up beside her, laying a hand on Martie's shoulder. "Wow, that's harsh. Are you okay?"

Martie found she'd been clutching the strap of her bag tight enough that she'd left fingernail marks in her palms. She forced herself to take a deep breath. "I just don't understand what this person is trying to do."

"Do you want me to go get a teacher?"

No doubt the school administration already knew. It was obvious—there was no writing on any other locker, and decorations were only allowed on the inside—and someone else would have seen and reported it, unless it just happened.

So maybe Ms. Molina *had* been in the classroom for her after all. Probably making sure that Martie had been accounted for the entire time.

"No, but thank you." Martie straightened her back and headed for her locker. Whether this was related to everything else or not, Martie was going to withstand it.

A little vandalism was the least of her problems at the moment, and maybe, like adults always said, if she ignored the bully, they would eventually get bored and turn their energies elsewhere.

Ms. Molina never came to talk to her, though. Hopefully that was because Martie was no longer considered a suspect, and she was looking elsewhere.

Though, if Martie were asked to give feedback on the scholarship experience, she would give the school negative marks for their handling of this particular situation.

That night, Martie had a series of strange dreams, which was nothing new. But it was new when she woke up and discovered she'd wandered outside in her sleep.

Outside, and into the graveyard.

It was frigid, and the cold instantly cut through her pajamas and bare feet. What in the world? She'd never sleepwalked, not that she'd been aware of, and no one in her family had ever mentioned it.

The ghost hung in the air in front of her. "It is almost time," she said. Martie blinked, and she had moved several feet closer to Martie, hovering over one of the gravestones. "I wonder where they will put you."

A chill that was not the cold cut through Martie. "Put me?"

The ghost stared past Martie, off toward the forest. "It awakens. It calls."

Come to me.

"It will take you," the ghost continued, "and then they will put you here, with the rest of us."

"Us?" Heart hammering, Martie reached out, running her fingers over the gravestone beneath the ghost. It was like touching ice, cold and smooth. "I don't understand."

"You won't get a gravestone." The ghost curled in on herself. "They'll just open the ground and put you in."

Martie resisted the urge to flee. Or to reach a hand out and see what she would find if she made contact. "Who are you?"

"I am who you will be." The ghost sighed, the sound more on the wind than real.

Martie's teeth began to chatter. "Are you saying…are you saying that you're a scholarship student?"

The ghost laughed, a harsh, haunted sound that echoed in Martie's soul. "They say not to look a gift horse in the mouth. But what if that horse is a Trojan horse?" She uncurled, drifting down to the ground, only inches from Martie.

Martie needed to go back inside before she froze. Or got frostbite. That was a thing, right, and not just a story someone had made up? Up above, the moon glowed low and full, casting a weird, too bright light over the landscape and creating shadows where they didn't make sense.

Maybe she wasn't awake. Maybe this was still a dream.

"What is your name?" Martie insisted. "Why do you linger?"

"I cannot pass on." The girl was fading now, being absorbed into the moonlight.

"Why not?"

The ghost said nothing, barely still there.

"Please don't go." Martie did reach out now, her fingers finding nothing. "Please, tell me who you are."

There was the faintest whisper on the wind. *Alice*.

Chapter Thirteen

MARTIE SHOT UP in her bed. It was still early, only the faintest light coming in through the skylight, and Hayden still slumbered peacefully. Martie ran her hands over her face. Everything felt normal.

So...it had been a dream? She sighed, flopping back down on the bed. Of course it was. A product of her own troubled psyche, trying to find answers where she had none. The scholarship students, buried out in the graveyard? Yeah, right. Her brain even knew that the family had been buried there before the school had been formed.

Well, a shower would get her mind off of that. Martie climbed down from bed but paused as her feet hit the floor. The bottoms of her pajama pants were wet.

Her heart skipped a beat. There was no way she could have gotten them wet in her bed. Which meant...

She knelt, feeling the carpet. From the door to the ladder of her bed was also damp. Just like someone had been outside, in bare feet in the dew, and had walked back inside and climbed back into bed.

Martie sat back on her heels and took several deep breaths, trying to calm her breathing and heart. It wasn't a dream.

Oh, Ms. Molina was going to have a field day with that, if/when she watched the security footage.

But if it wasn't a dream...

Martie crept over to her desk and slid open the lowest drawer, the one she'd been storing the folders from the archives in. She dug out the original folder, the one with George, and Alice, and Donna.

She hadn't been able to find anything out about Alice. There was just this one picture. Martie laid it on her desk, trying to reconcile the living, smiling girl in it with the phantom that had haunted her since her arrival. She tried to add eyes into where the ghost only had holes with limited success. Maybe.

Hayden's words floated back to her. It could be a demon, taking on human form to lure her into...something. Whatever it was that lurked in the woods. But why?

And it hadn't really been luring, had it? Martie ran back over the haunting in her mind. No, no luring. If anything, the ghost had been trying to scare her off. She'd thought it was because she was a scholarship student, and the ghost didn't approve of letting in common riffraff, but if the ghost was Alice, if she'd been a scholarship student herself…

…then she knew what happened to the scholarship students, because it had happened to her, and she'd been trying to get Martie to leave since she'd arrived.

The ghost had been protecting her. Trying to warn her.

But warn her of what?

Martie packed up the file again and went to take her shower. She turned the water up hot, almost scalding, and let it run over her, trying to let the heat burn away everything. All right, what did she know?

Not a single scholarship student had finished their time at Greyson Academy. They'd all come here, probably overjoyed at the opportunity, dreaming of what they'd accomplished in the future, and they'd all vanished. But not the same way—George Miller had run off to join the military, someone else had been pregnant and asked to leave, according to Mr. Brooks, et cetera. The kids they'd gone to school with hadn't realized that they'd disappeared, just that they left the school, and as far as Martie knew, no one had ever come to the school to figure out where their missing child had gone.

If she hadn't dreamed last night, the scholarship students were all dead, buried in the graveyard. No gravestones, Alice had said. So someone concocted a reason for them to leave, killed them, and buried them?

Why?

Why have scholarship students just to kill them off?

This line of thought had dead ended. Martie shifted her focus to her parents. Alice said she couldn't pass on. And Hayden, too, had pointed out how it was a good thing that she couldn't contact her parents. If Alice really was Alice, she was a former shadow of what she must have been in life. Did Martie want that for her parents? To have them doomed to wander the earth, colorless and featureless?

No, of course not.

Martie closed her eyes and let the water wash over her. She pictured her parents, as she had so often recently, smiling and happy, reaching out for her.

I love you, she told them in her mind, *and I will never stop missing you. Goodbye, for now.*

She let the image fade, like they were going to a better place, and all the other trite things people said when someone you loved died. And she cried, tears mixing with the steaming water. It was like she'd released something inside of her, something she'd bottled up and locked away, and now it was all coming out, whether she wanted it to or not. Her heart felt hollow, her insides raw.

I love you, she said over and over, like a mantra.

It wasn't fair. She'd never had much, but she'd had her parents, and together, they had been enough. They'd made good times out of the rough, and she'd never doubted their love for her. And they were gone, had been taken from her in a split second.

Part of her wished she'd gone too, just so she didn't have to deal with the pain that coursed through her now.

But she hadn't. And her parents wouldn't want her to have lived only to succumb to whatever now.

The safe thing to do would be to leave. To call Aunt Jessica and head back to Arizona. But she suspected that she wouldn't make it. That that would be the excuse she left behind, like George Miller wanting to join the war effort. Everyone would think she'd just gone home, too traumatized by her parents' death to keep going here at Greyson, and in reality, she'd have met the same fate as the other scholarship students and be buried in the graveyard.

No gravestone. Probably in case someone was keeping count. No new gravestones in a graveyard that in theory hadn't been touched in over a century.

Okay, so where did that leave her? She couldn't run, not anymore. That was probably why the hauntings had decreased over time, not the pendant or the keyhole, since the ghost was still showing up all over the place.

Alice had tried to scare her away while there was still time, and now it was too late.

Well, if she couldn't escape, she'd have to figure out what the danger was and get around it somehow. Alice would know, but if Martie's attempts to contact her parents had taught her anything, she knew zilch about communicating with the spirits. And Alice had never been terribly forthcoming with answers, when she answered Martie's questions at all.

Alice had been trying to help her this whole time, though, from trying to get her to leave to providing useful information from the archives. Martie would need to be on the lookout, see if she was leaving more clues.

And she'd need to do it fast. *It awakens*, Alice had said. *It calls*.

Martie turned off the water and stepped out of the shower into the chill a room takes when you've been somewhere warm and now are not. Light was just starting to filter in from outside, a flat, gray light that brought no cheer or hope with it.

"Alice?" Martie called, but quietly, in case someone else—someone alive—was in the room somewhere.

But there was no answer, living or dead. The lights stayed on, and no one stood at the edges of her vision.

"Alice," Martie said again, feeling ridiculous. "Can you tell me what is out there? What happened to you? To all of you?"

Again, nothing. Martie stood as still as she could, towel pulled loosely around her body, listening as if that one intention could bring her the answers she needed. But all she got was goosebumps and water on the floor. There was nothing, not even a shift in the air, that would imply that Alice was there.

It figured. She hadn't been able to get rid of the girl forever, and now she was nowhere to be found.

Hayden was awake when Martie got back, mostly dressed and in the process of braiding her long, blonde hair into a single plait down the back. "Good morning," she said when Martie came in, though there was some weird undercurrent to her voice. "How'd you sleep?"

Martie picked out some school clothes—tights, skirt, sweater, blouse—and laid them over the back of her desk chair. "Not great," she answered. "I think...I think I may have sleepwalked. Did you hear me at all? Or, like, the door opening?"

Hayden glanced over her shoulder at Martie, concern written across her face. "You were sleepwalking? That's got to be wildly dangerous. What if you'd gone over the railing?" She finished her braid and wrapped a hair tie around the end. "You've got to see someone about this, Martie. I'm worried about you."

"But you didn't hear anything?"

"Martie, you know how heavy I sleep."

It was true. Hayden would probably sleep through a fire alarm, if one went off. "I was outside, in the graveyard, with the ghost—or I dreamed I was. My pants were wet when I got up this morning." Martie picked them up from where'd she'd left them when she'd left for the bathroom, but they were dry now, and any wetness in the carpet could be attributed to the fact that she'd just come back from the shower.

Hayden took a deep breath. "Martie," she said, very seriously, "I need you to talk to someone. I'm worried about you."

She doesn't believe me. Not that Martie blamed her. How must this all look from Hayden's point of view? She gets some weird scholarship student as a roommate, and said roommate starts asking about hauntings and claiming she sees a ghost girl that no one else ever sees. And yes, maybe she can go along with the idea for a bit, because the lights do flicker and doors do occasionally close by themselves, but as time goes on, the roommate's claims get weirder and more distressing, and you learn that her parents recently died and that she blocked the fact that she was with them when they died from her memory.

Plus, the whole thing with the vandalism and the fact that Martie had been obsessed with the other scholarship students. Hayden was absolutely right to believe that Martie was making everything up—oh, not on purpose, Hayden would never think something mean like that—and was mentally disturbed.

Not for the first time, and probably not for the last, Martie stopped to consider whether or not she was, indeed, crazy, suffering from a mental break from her parents' deaths and her own near-death experience.

She didn't think so. Of course, probably every crazy person thought that. But really everything came down to this: if she were crazy and she continued to look into the scholarship students and what happened to them, things were unlikely to get worse. But if she wasn't crazy, and something *was* happening to the scholarship students, and she didn't do anything to prepare, well, she was as doomed as all the ones who had come before her.

But she could leave Hayden out of it.

Hayden was still watching her, her face carefully blank. Hayden had protected her thus far, but that probably wouldn't last, not if Hayden was beginning to think Martie could be capable of destroying things.

"I'll think about it," Martie said. She focused on getting dressed and ready, and Hayden didn't say anything else the entire time.

A thick layer of dew hung on everything outside—another thing that hardly ever happened in Arizona—despite the temperature having to be close to freezing. Martie pulled her coat closed even more at the throat, practically choking herself. It didn't help.

As she peered across the grass toward the graveyard, trying to see if she could make out her own footprints in the dew, she felt it again, but lighter. The pull from the forest. There were no words, no commands. More like a light prodding, just checking whether or not she was there.

She was not crazy. She couldn't afford to be.

They filed into Mrs. Weissman's classroom and took their seats. Martie fished her laptop out of her bag automatically and opened it up to her notes for today's presentation. Someone had filled in the scratches in the table with wood putty, but you could still make out the words if you squinted. Still, an improvement.

"Good morning," Mrs. Weissman said, standing up as soon as they were all seated. "Who would like to go first?"

Sinclair's hand shot up, and she stood before Mrs. Weissman had even acknowledged her. "I've done my research on evil forests," she said in a clear, confident voice, meeting the eyes of everyone around the table. Someone who was practiced in public speaking. Who thrived in it. No doubt that would be an asset to her family and their business.

What did Sinclair's family do? She had no idea.

Maybe they really did run the gas station chain.

"An interesting aspect that is related to the idea of evil forests," Sinclair was saying, "is the connected idea of a forest guardian." She paused to tilt her computer screen, probably so she could see it better while she was standing. "Forest guardians are found in cultures across the world. The details vary, but, in general, a forest guardian protects all or part of a forest, which is generally healthier than the surrounding landscape or, in some cases, considered to be magical or have magical properties." She looked up, meeting Martie's gaze and holding it. "These guardians are said to be fiercely protective of their territory and the creatures and plants within it, and they will attack and, in many cases, kill anyone who causes any damage or other hurtful circumstance."

Why was Sinclair staring at her?

"Very good observation. Does anyone have anything to add to this forest guardian topic?" Mrs. Weissman asked.

Several people did. Sinclair sat down while the discussion rang, though her eyes never left Martie.

Seriously, why was she staring? Was she trying to intimidate Martie? Get her to add in her two cents?

She didn't have any. They didn't have forests or forest guardians where she lived, and local folklore tended more toward skinwalkers and other things that lurked in the desert.

Sinclair finally got pulled into a discussion with someone else about whether or not forest guardians could be considered evil. Martie breathed a sigh of relief.

The rest of the class flew by. They didn't actually have to present all their research, just whatever they felt was most interesting, or something new if someone else had researched the same topic, and then everyone was free to comment or discuss that information. Sinclair did spend a lot of time watching Martie, but not with the same intensity as she had earlier.

Weird girl.

In math, Martie found another note, in that same handwriting, in her bag.

Why did no one come looking after they disappeared?

Hm. Cryptic and unhelpful.

But the question haunted her through math and chemistry. Why hadn't anyone come looking for the scholarship students after they'd disappeared? She'd run over the possibilities before, everything from the school paying the family to keep quiet to families looking elsewhere due to the covers each student's disappearance was seemingly given. But this implied that no one came looking.

Why not?

The answer was almost there. She could feel it on the cusp of forming, sitting in the shadows of her thoughts.

She'd go back to her room, during lunch, and look at the file again. She had to be missing something.

Also, who was just slipping notes into her bag? Why couldn't they come talk to her? They obviously knew something and wanted to help, and it was just getting ridiculous at this point.

Hayden was still being distant. She waited for Martie as chemistry ended, but she kept fidgeting, like she wanted to go and was forcing herself to stay.

Martie needed to get this figured out so she could fix things with Hayden. And, you know, not disappear.

"Martina, a moment, please," Mr. Brooks said as she reached the door.

Martie closed her eyes and took a deep breath, remembering last week's disastrous conversation. "Go on without me," she said to Hayden. This would probably take a while. Maybe she could just agree to see the counselor a couple times a week and head off everything else.

When she opened her eyes, Hayden was already gone.

Great.

As she stepped back into the classroom, Mr. Brooks added, "Close the door, please."

Oh, this was really not going to go well. Martie did so, trying to keep her face carefully neutral. "Yes, Mr. Brooks?"

"I was hoping you could explain these to me." Mr. Brooks opened his desk and pulled out several sheets of paper. "If you're asking for help, I'm afraid I may not be the right person in this case."

"Asking for help?" Martie took several steps closer, craning her head to better see the pages as Mr. Brooks spread them across his desk. They were drawings, but disturbing ones, the sort that people used to joke about how creepy children could be. Dark figures, blood, things crawling out of the dark. "I don't understand."

Mr. Brooks flipped one of the sheets over. There, on the back, was sprawled the same handwriting that was following her throughout the school. *The dark is closing in*, it read. *It's getting closer.* And then, of course, signed with her name.

"I did not make these," Martie said as firmly as she could. "It's whoever is trying to get me kicked out of school."

Mr. Brooks folded his hands on top of a picture that was mostly scribbled black except for a small, white figure in the middle. It made Martie think of Alice, floating alone over the graveyard. "Martina, I admit that I didn't think you capable of the vandalism in Mrs. Weissman's classroom based on your behavior in my class and the conversations I've had with you, but these pictures are very worrying. If you're having dark thoughts like this—which would be completely understandable, based on your recent tragedies—you need to get professional help. I believe our school counselor will be able to pull in an additional, external professional if necessary."

He kept talking, but Martie tuned him out, focusing on her supposed "letter." The handwriting was vaguely familiar, but not something she could immediately identify. A heavy feeling of dread settled deep inside. This was never going to stop. She was going to wake up or come into school every day, or almost every day, and find something new that she apparently did, until it wasn't just Hayden and Mr. Brooks who had given up on her, but everyone. And even if she didn't disappear, she would never be able to rebuild those relationships or her position in this school.

It wasn't Alice doing this; Martie was absolutely certain of that now. So it had to be someone else, someone alive. Someone alive, who was either creating the cover for when she disappeared, or who merely wanted her kicked out. Neither was a good alternative.

"Okay, Martina?" Mr. Brooks said, cutting through her thoughts.

Martie nodded hesitantly. "Can I go?"

Mr. Brooks had begun gathering the drawings back up. "Yes, of course."

Martie didn't look back. She jumped down the stairs and barely remembered to put her coat on before she ducked outside. It had begun to precipitate, a weird mix between rain and snow that stung her cheeks as she ran back to the dorm. Her file was where she'd left it. Martie dropped her bag onto the floor and sat down heavily as she flipped through the pages inside. What was she missing?

Her fingers lingered on Donna's diary again. Martie re-read it once more. It was just…day-to-day stuff. Donna had felt the same things Martie had on her acceptance to Greyson. Relief at leaving a not-good home environment, excitement at the opportunity to get ahead.

Wait.

Donna talked about leaving her foster family. Which meant, like Martie, she didn't have parents. Or, at least, she didn't have parents who could take care of her.

Martie pulled her laptop out of her bag and ran her searches again on anyone who had come up with actual, useful information.

That was the trend. Each scholarship student came from a broken home of some sort. Most had lost at least one parent, if not both, and others had been living in less-than-ideal situations. Each news article, no matter its decade or location, had to point out how great it was for that child to be the one to receive the scholarship, how awful their lives had been before.

No one had come looking, because there was no one to come.

The scholarship students are needed, that one note had said. And now it seemed they were purposefully chosen to be the sort of person no one would miss when they vanished. Someone was seeking out students for something, making sure the disappearances would go unnoticed, and they'd been doing it for over a century.

Her stomach grumbled. Damn, she was going to miss lunch again, and she really shouldn't. She'd noticed that her clothes were starting to hang loosely, which probably wasn't helping her look like the sort of not-crazy, not-depressed person who definitely would not disappear one of these days. She slipped the file back into its drawer and her laptop back into her bag. If she hurried, she should be able to grab something, and Miss Towers, her Classical Literature teacher, tended to look the other way if people snacked in class.

Alice hung outside her door, waiting.

She was outside the railing, floating near the top of the atrium.

"You have death on you," Alice said. "That's why I can see you."

She'd said that before. Was that part of it? Not just that people wouldn't be missed, but people who had almost died or been strongly affected by someone else's death? Something that allowed Martie to see Alice, and Alice to see her.

"What's waiting in the woods?" Martie asked, tightening her grip on her bag.

"Pain," Alice said, and faded away.

Martie stared at where she'd been. Stupid, unhelpful ghost. Stupid, unhelpful note leaver.

Martie forced herself to run to lunch and managed to snag a grilled cheese sandwich and a bag of chips.

In Classical Literature, they were watching the movie version of *Much Ado About Nothing*, which had more nudity than Martie had expected from a

Shakespeare play—or a movie that they'd watch in school. Miss Towers slipped her a juice box once the room was dark.

Martie tried to focus on the movie but found herself doodling across her notes instead. Ghosts, and trees, and a dark figure in them. Man, if Mr. Brooks saw these, her case for not doing the other ones was essentially shot. Maybe she could point out that the handwriting wasn't hers.

She suspected what Mr. Brooks thought was one of the least of her problems.

What was in the woods? What would happen when it was ready for her, when she wouldn't be able to resist its call anymore?

Would Aunt Jessica come looking when she disappeared? Or would she accept the school's excuse, that Martie had been depressed and not dealing well with her parents' deaths and the relocation to effing Vermont, and had disappeared into the forest of her own volition?

The worst thing was, Aunt Jessica probably would. Martie had repressed her own memory of being in the accident and the hospital, and had refused to talk about her parents at all the entire time she'd been living with Aunt Jessica. Those were not things well-adjusted people did. Martie had thought Aunt Jessica had also been avoiding the subject, but maybe her aunt was just doing it for her sake.

And here at school, too, people would totally buy it. Martie could picture Hayden whispering to other people about how Martie had been claiming to be haunted, and hearing voices, and had become increasingly paranoid.

The situation was set, and Martie had played right into it. Or maybe they'd built it based off of Martie herself once she'd arrived.

If she packed up in the night and left, would she actually get anywhere? Or just disappear sooner than predicted?

God, it was so cold. She'd probably freeze to death before anything else. Who invented this weather? It sucked.

Maybe...maybe the solution was to face things head-on. If she knew what was in the woods—besides pain, thanks, Alice—perhaps she would be able to put together some sort of defense.

Today was Friday. Tomorrow, she could hike into the woods and see what there was to see. Students weren't really supposed to leave campus for any reason to avoid distractions and bad influences, but Martie had noticed a few trails leading into the woods, and Hayden had mentioned that sometimes classes took nature hikes for whatever reason. She'd brought her old backpack, not knowing they were going to give her a new bag here, and had water bottles for martial arts. She'd just need to pack layers and extra food from breakfast, and she should be good, at least for a few hours.

She'd hiked back in Arizona, in the cooler months. The first rule of hiking was not to do it alone, and to make sure someone knew where you'd been planning on going, in case something happened to you, but it would probably be best to forego both of those. If nothing happened, and she made it back to school, hopefully with useful information, the last thing she needed was to get in trouble for being in the woods.

Besides, who would she tell, or ask to go with her? Hayden already thought she was crazy, and Martie'd been so distracted with the haunting and everything that while she was friendly with some people, she wouldn't call them friends.

Also, what if she ran into whatever lurked in the woods and inadvertently led someone else to whatever fate awaited her? Yeah, no, it was best to just go.

No more waiting. She was going to take her fate into her own hands.

At least, as much as she could.

Chapter Fourteen

MARTIE LAID HER haul out on the floor of her room. Two turkey sandwiches, a bag of chips, several muffins, two bananas, three granola bars, and a Rice Krispie treat. The kitchen workers had been oddly enthusiastic about making sure she got enough to eat. Maybe her clothes were fitting worse than she'd thought.

But, anyway, that should be enough to get through, well, at least the day. Martie stuffed it all into her backpack on top of her hat, gloves, another coat, and two sweaters. She didn't think she'd be out overnight, but she didn't really have anything that would work in that situation anyway.

Hayden had gone out, which was just as well. Martie didn't want to explain what she was doing.

Slinging her backpack over her warmest coat, Martie slid on a pair of gloves and a wool hat and headed out. She half-expected Alice to be waiting to say something unhelpful and cryptic, but the ghost was nowhere in sight. Was that a good or a bad thing? Martie didn't know anymore.

People were about inside, but once she got outside, there was hardly anyone. It wasn't that awful of a day, not that Martie had seen, anyway. The sun was bright and there wasn't a cloud in the sky, even though it was still unreasonably cold. Martie marched across the lawn to where one of the trails led down the side of the hill.

She'd considered going through the graveyard, as some sort of symbolism, but had thought better of it.

The forest rose up immediately once she left the hilltop. The trees were skeletons of themselves, their empty branches reaching up toward the sun. Their former leaves lay in thick layers on the ground, some still retaining their brilliance, others rotting and turning brown. It was weirdly quiet, too—no animals, no wind. Martie readjusted her bag and took a deep breath. It looked like a normal forest. Maybe it was just a normal forest, and she'd made a conspiracy out of nothing.

Well, only one way to find out.

The trail was fairly thin, only wide enough for Martie, and snaked back and forth across the face of the hill on the opposite side from the road. Without their leaves, the trees let in plenty of light. Still, shouldn't there be birds? Maybe not. Birds flew south for the winter, right? And animals hibernated. While it wasn't technically winter yet, Martie didn't blame the animals if they'd decided it was.

It took close to an hour to make it to the forest floor. Martie stared back up toward the school, but all there was to see was the naked trees, some boulders, and the occasional bush, half of which had dropped their leaves, and the other half of which had tried to hang on to them. The resulting leaves were sickly and drab, not looking much better than the rotting leaves on the ground. The hill rose into the air high above her, and there was no sign of the school, or its manicured lawns, or anybody else.

Okay, great. She was in the woods. Now what?

Martie spun in a slow circle, staring deeper into the undergrowth. Aside from the hill, everything was the same. Dead trees, dying leaves, quiet, no animals. Nothing called out to her or tugged at her, and there was no indication of a direction to go aside from the path, continuing to wend its way deeper.

Well, that was as good as any, she supposed. After taking a moment to get some water and eat part of the Rice Krispie treat, Martie headed along it. The path down here was muddy in places, sucking at her boots, but not insistently. Martie kept peering into the woods, looking for something that would illuminate the supposed conspiracy here. Something like, oh, hanging figures made out of sticks, or symbols carved into the trees. Weird dead spots where nothing grew. Blood staining the rocks.

Martie suspected she watched too many movies.

The path ran more or less parallel to the hill itself, wrapping slowly around the base. Maybe it went back up again on the other side by the road.

She continued on. It was a nice enough hike, she guessed, but she was starting to feel a little silly. It had seemed so obvious, back up at the school, to think that the woods hid something evil, some cult or something. It was so many trees—who knew what they hid? But now that she was down here, inside it, it was just...normal. Or, at least, what she assumed was normal for this sort of forest, having never been in one before. In movies and books, evil forests were always dark and misty.

The sunlight, if anything, had gotten brighter.

Off to Martie's right and a little ways ahead was a large boulder, climbing maybe twenty feet up the side of the hill. It had a nice, flat top to it. Martie should climb up there, have a snack, and see if anything was noticeable from a higher elevation. Not that she expected there would be—she'd been higher earlier and despite the trees' lack of leaves, they still did a pretty decent job of blocking the view.

Behind her, something cracked.

Martie spun around. All right, this was it. Something *was* in this forest, and now it was coming up behind Martie, and goddamnit, she was going to see what it was and fight it off or die trying.

Sinclair crashed into view, several sticks and leaves stuck in her hair. She was not dressed for a hike at all besides a heavy coat, and her white tights were stained with mud.

Okay, this was not what Martie had expected. "Sinclair?"

"Are you freaking *crazy?*" Sinclair slid to a stop in front of her and tried unsuccessfully to pull out a couple of the sticks. "Why would you willingly come in here?"

"Why wouldn't I?" Martie dug out one of her water bottles and offered it, but Sinclair waved it away. "It's just a forest."

"Just a forest?" Sinclair's voice reached a painful pitch. "Just a *forest?* Have you not been listening to anything I've said?"

Anything she'd said? Martie frowned, running over all the conversations she and the other girl had had. There'd been nothing about forests, except for her presentation in Comparative History. "I don't understand."

Sinclair successfully removed a few of the leaves. "I was looking right at you. I know you were paying attention."

"Did you…did you run straight down the hill?"

"Martie, focus!" Sinclair pinched the bridge of her nose.

Martie took another deep breath. Sinclair's presentation had been on forest guardians. "Forest guardians are good things, I thought. They protect their parts of the forest and keep them from harm."

"They also hate outsiders." Sinclair must have decided to give up on her hair, because she smoothed it with her hand and finally stopped fussing with it. "Especially humans, because humans almost always cause harm."

"So? It's not like they're real. It's just stories, based on a few half-remembered experiences people had forever ago."

Sinclair gave her a look, like she was being especially obtuse. "It's not real? Just like your ghost friend isn't real, I suppose."

Martie froze. "My ghost friend?" Sinclair could see Alice? What did that mean? "How long…?"

"How long have I've known about her? It's not like she's subtle." Sinclair crossed her arms over her chest.

"Though until you showed up, she mostly stood in corridors, silently watching."

This was…this was fantastic. Martie hadn't imagined Alice. Not unless Sinclair was also imagining her, which seemed unlikely. Martie couldn't imagine Sinclair putting up with anything so inconvenient as visual hallucinations.

Wait. Alice was not in question here.

"Are you saying there is a forest guardian? Right here?" Martie turned in a circle, peering into the forest once more. When she reached the hillside again, she stopped. Where the large boulder had been, the one she'd debated eating atop of, there was now a cave entrance instead, the same height that the boulder had been. "Do you see that?"

Sinclair grabbed her arm. "We need to get out of here."

"No." Sinclair was strong, but Martie managed to stand her ground. "You know what's happening here, don't you?"

"Martie, *come on*."

"Sinclair, I'm going to *die* soon if I can't figure this out."

Sinclair stopped yanking, despair painting her face. "I know."

The validation of her fears was unexpected. Martie's knees went weak, so she allowed herself to sink to the ground, into the mud and the rotting leaves. "Have you been leaving the folders on the scholarship students in the archives?"

"Do you have them?" Sinclair sat down on her knees beside Martie. Her tights were never going to be clean again. "My father started putting them together when he went here, and I've been working on them, too. I couldn't figure out where they'd gone. I was worried…" She trailed off, gazing seriously at Martie. "What do you know?"

"I know that the scholarship students are specifically picked because no one would come looking for them when they disappeared. Or because they'd put together some sort of reasonable explanation as to why they disappeared. Something people wouldn't question." Martie took a deep breath. "They're spread out so that the disappearances aren't an obvious trend. And there's something about…something about them being affected by death."

"You're close." Sinclair pried the water bottle out of Martie's hand and took a sip. "The spacing isn't to throw off suspicion about the disappearances. The interval is because the scholarship students are needed at very specific times."

The scholarship students are needed. That's what the note had said. "You're the one leaving notes in my bag, aren't you?"

Sinclair nodded.

"What are they—we—needed for?"

Without a word, Sinclair waved at the cave.

"The forest guardian? I don't understand."

Sinclair wrung her hands. "There's a pattern. My family has been coming to Greyson since the beginning, and from what I understand, the beginning was rough. And then, all of a sudden, things fixed themselves. At least, that's what my," she paused to count on her fingers, "great-great-great grandfather wrote in his diaries. Things would randomly break or disappear, people would get ill or hurt, the buildings themselves seemed to be plagued with creaking and poor construction. And then, one day, it all stopped. The day after the first scholarship student disappeared."

"Donald Cooper."

"Yes. After things stopped falling apart, the school started to do quite well. My great-great-great grandfather was asked to serve on the board. But after a while, things started to get spotty again. Not like they had, but enough that my great-great-great grandfather, remembering his days at school, noticed. But, then, another student disappeared."

That must have been George Miller. "They said he'd run off to join the war effort."

"Right, that one." Sinclair swallowed. "In his journals, my...ancestor...expressed his disbelief in that story. He noted how when he talked to the student's friends, they'd noted that he'd started acting strangely the last week or so before he left. Talked about hearing voices and being called to the woods. But the war effort story also had merit, as the student had also expressed an interest in being of help, and none of the other board members were concerned. Nor did any of the boy's family come forward to challenge the official story. But after that...things got better again."

Martie frowned at the ground. The cold from the mud seeped through her pants, and her legs felt stiff and frozen. So the students disappeared, and the school prospered. Until it didn't, and then the whole thing repeated itself. "So, the forest guardian...doesn't like the school being here?" That made sense, as much as any of this did, if she accepted that the guardian was real. If this was its cave, that made the hill its home.

And this hill was weird. She'd thought that when she arrived. There were no other hills, not like this, anywhere nearby.

"Why not just tell me this?" Martie asked. "Why the notes and the cryptic messages? And I flat out asked you about the other scholarship students, and you lied to me."

"I'm really sorry," Sinclair said, and seemed sincere. "But can you imagine? If I just came up to you out of nowhere and told you needed to leave because you would be sacrificed to a forest guardian so the school would be allowed to remain and prosper?"

She was right. Martie would have thought she was crazy, especially when she'd first arrived, or thought Sinclair was just trying to get rid of her because she didn't fit into the rich kid mold of everyone else. And then she'd been so focused on the haunting.

"What do I do?" she asked out loud. "It's too late for me to leave. They've got the whole thing set up, where they've made me look unstable and depressive. I've heard something calling in the woods. It's got to be almost time. How do I fight this? How do I stop this?"

Sinclair paled. "I don't know."

"You don't know?" Martie could hear the panic in her own voice. "I thought you guys had this all figured out."

"We've been working on it!" Sinclair hauled herself to her feet, pacing back and forth. "We've got the pattern of the problems and the disappearances, and someone along the way connected in ancient stories from the native people of the guardian in this area. But none of us have ever seen the guardian. We don't know how the agreement between the school and the guardian works, if there even is one. And we don't know who picks the scholarship students or how they know when it's time to."

This new information wasn't worth anything. Anger pooled in Martie's stomach. She, too, pushed to her feet, her pants cracking under the mud. "Well, I know of one way to find out."

"What?" Sinclair shook her head. "Oh, no, Martie, you can't go in there!"

"What am I supposed to do? Just wait until it calls me and it's too late? No, screw that." Tears pricked the corners of her eyes. "I have already lost so much. If I die now, at least I do it on my own terms. At least I go in and face things while I still have the capacity to do so." She grabbed both of Sinclair's hands in her own. "Promise me, Sinclair. Promise me you'll fight back against the image they've painted of me. Promise me you'll figure out what's going on here."

Sinclair sniffed, tears pooling in her own eyes. "I promise. Good…good luck."

Martie turned to face the cave. What sort of creature needed such a large entrance? It took several deep breaths before she could force her feet to move. What had happened to the boulder? Had something moved it? Had it been an illusion?

She hated this. Why couldn't everything just be as it had been? She didn't need anything supernatural in her life.

Behind her, Sinclair sniffled, but Martie kept her shoulders straight, her path forward moving. She paused just outside the cave, took another deep breath and, before her brain could catch up, took a step inside.

Chapter Fifteen

THE LIGHT FROM outside illuminated maybe thirty feet into the cave. It…it looked like a normal cave, or at least how she'd seen caves in movies and pictures and what have you, stone and dirt mixing near the entrance before grayish-tan stone continued unevenly farther back. She wasn't sure what she had expected. Bones, maybe. Blood. Something that implied the danger that lurked inside.

If it lurked inside.

What was definitely true was that she was likely to walk into a stone wall or trip over a stalactite and die without a flashlight or something. Stalactite? Stalagmite. She didn't have any idea. Something.

Martie inched her way inside. She should go outside and find a flashlight somewhere, but Sinclair would be out there, still, and what would she think when Martie came back out? And for something as stupid as a flashlight?

She was aware that what Sinclair thought in this situation should not have mattered, and yet, here she was.

Her foot hit something metallic, which bounced farther into the cave. Martie bent down, searching with her hands, and grabbed when her fingers hit cold metal. It was an ancient, massive flashlight, and had to weigh at least a couple of pounds.

It had probably been down here for decades. Had one of her predecessors brought it, not knowing their fate? Or perhaps when they'd been drawn here to their doom. Or maybe it belonged to whoever selected the scholarship students, knowing they'd be led to this eventually. Maybe they came each time, to make sure the deed was done.

Alice had said they were all buried in the graveyard, after all. Someone would have to retrieve what was left.

All right, enough of *that* train of thought.

Martie swallowed around her suddenly dry throat and flicked the switch on the flashlight. It spluttered out half a second of light before giving up.

Martie banged it across her hand a couple of times before smacking it against the cave wall. The rock gave before the flashlight, but it did, after a moment, flicker into dim life. It didn't help much, but it was something.

Man, they really didn't make things like they used to. What did this thing run on? Sheer will?

Despite the mud and obvious water, the rock itself wasn't that slippery. Martie continued back, shining the flashlight about and hoping it would last. It continued to just be...a cave. There was water dripping somewhere, slow and echoing, and no clear path, but the cave itself was narrow and straight, almost like a tunnel.

It was warmer in the cave than it had been outside. Martie peeled off her coat and took a moment to stuff it into her backpack and have a quick snack. She tried not to think of the sandwich as her last meal.

What was she doing? What if this was just a cave?

But she hadn't imagined that boulder. She knew she hadn't. She'd stared at it for quite a while. It hadn't been a trick of the light, and boulders that size didn't just disappear on their own. Or ever.

The cave continued on. Martie could no longer see the entrance, not even as a pinpoint of light.

Okay. She'd give it a little longer, and then she'd go back out. And then what? If this cave had no answers, where did that leave her?

Nowhere good, that was where.

Up ahead, the cave widened, the ceiling and walls disappearing from the sphere of Martie's light. Martie slowed, shining the flashlight about, but aside from the floor—which had quite a bit more water here—she couldn't make out anything.

Going into the water seemed like a bad idea. She'd freeze if she got her clothes wet, especially if this cave plan went nowhere. But if she didn't, this seemed to be the end of the line.

Deeper, in the dark, something moved.

Martie froze, pointing her light toward the noise, though of course that helped not at all. "Hello?" she called, then immediately wished she hadn't. Clutching the flashlight tightly, she waited.

Nothing. Not even more movement. Well, at least, not movement she could hear.

This was stupid. She was stupid. What had she been thinking? She'd get out of here; she'd call her aunt. If nothing else, Aunt Jessica would know that Martie hadn't disappeared on purpose.

Unless, of course, the school spun the story that Martie had become delusional and paranoid as part of her mental break.

God, this sucked so much.

This is new, said the voice in her head. *You are early. It is not yet time.*

Ice crawled through Martie's veins. Oh, heavens, this was a million times worse than being in the dark and thinking she was wasting her time. The voice was ancient, commanding, and who knew what sort of being it actually belonged to. "Look," she said. "I don't know what's going on here, but I want you to know that I do not consent to…whatever it is. It is not fair to bring people here under false pretenses, to give them hope, and then destroy them. Find someone else. Leave me alone."

The voice laughed, a low, rumbly tone that echoed through Martie's bones. *Consent? What makes you think I care about your consent?*

"It's an easy out." Anger rose through Martie. "Why do you let the people you made whatever bargain with not give anything they actually care about?"

The laughter stopped. *Elaborate.*

Martie clung to her little circle of light, trying to figure out where in the dark the guardian was. "First, tell me the details of your bargain with the school."

You are not in a position to make demands.

"Am I not?" The light around Martie shook with her hands. She swallowed. "Do I not deserve to know what I'm going to die for?"

There was silence from the dark. Martie pointed her ancient flashlight back down at the water and tried to decide how deep it was—or how far it went—but the light barely reflected off the surface. It was just a black maw, waiting to swallow her up.

Besides, apparently she was close enough.

They violated the sanctuary of my forest, the voice finally said. *They came, and they cleared away all the trees, and they destroyed them to build their own place. A place they thought nature could not touch. But my reach is far, and my power is vast.* It sounded almost…smug. *Many of them died. I thought they would go, then, but they didn't, clinging to the land. If anything, more of them came, multiplying, doing what they would against my will.* Anger now, echoing through the essence of the words.

"Why not just…kill them all?" Martie asked, shining her light ineffectively into the cavern. She sensed movement, somewhere outside of sight, but it did not seem close.

I am not cruel. Now it sounded offended. Great. *I gave them every opportunity to make the right decision. But then they came to me. Asked to stay. Said that, in exchange, they would make a sacrifice in my honor whenever I demanded it. And they have held up their end of the bargain. Each time I wake, someone has been ready for my taking. Or, if not, they prepare them quickly enough. In exchange, I have allowed their occupation of my sacred hill and given them what luck I could.*

Martie had so many questions. Yes, the scholarship students were selected, chosen so their disappearances would be masked and unquestioned, but how did the forest guardian—or whatever it was—know which child was to be the sacrifice? If there was an element of death involved, where someone had touched death or whatever it was that Alice had said, there was no guarantee that only the scholarship student would have that quality. After all, Sinclair could see Alice too.

You are early, the voice said again, *but I am ready to accept you.*

The motion in the dark that Martie sensed drifted closer, sending the water splashing against the walls or rocks or something. Martie lurched back as it approached, still seeing nothing in her feeble light, but sensing something huge overhead, staring down at her.

"No, wait!" She swallowed, clutching the flashlight like it might, conceivably, be used as a weapon. "That's what I mean. They promised to sacrifice to you, in your honor, right? But they're not."

You have come. They have come before you.

"Sure, they're sending people," Martie said. "But not people they care about. Someone came to you, right, and said they'd send you a sacrifice? But they're picking out people from elsewhere and bringing them here just to get rid of them. People they figure no one will miss. Not people they care about. It's no sacrifice to the people on top of the hill if you take the person they offer. They can just find another one, whenever they want, and lure them here with promises of success, and then give them to you whenever you ask."

And wasn't that just like the rich? To solve a problem by climbing over the people they deemed beneath them. Martie could just picture it, some old, white robber baron type, in a waistcoat with a pocket watch, standing here and promising a sacrifice, knowing he'd never dare touch one of the students who'd come to the school on their own but that he could go to any gutter anywhere and find someone who'd beg him to take them. He must have been so damn proud of himself, finding a way to subdue the forest guardian at very little cost to himself.

There was silence from the cavern and Martie's brain. Then a roar started low within the ground, growing and echoing, shaking the cavern around her. Martie cowered, holding both hands over her head, like that would do anything when the hill fell down.

How dare they trick me! Something large crashed within the cavern. Martie flattened herself against the cave wall and closed her eyes. *I will destroy them. I will tear down their unholy buildings, and I will suck their souls dry. I will make them rue the day they touched my forest and my hill.*

If whatever he was doing didn't stop, the whole hill was coming down, and the school would definitely be destroyed. But…that wasn't fair, either. Did everyone at the school deserve to die for something some asshole over a hundred years ago had done? Did Hayden deserve to die? Sinclair? Noor? Even Winchester? No. If what Sinclair had said was true—and Martie suspected it was—there were only a few people at the school who knew of the bargain and selected the students for sacrifice. Had selected Martie to be sacrificed. But other than that...everyone was innocent. They didn't deserve to die for this.

"Wait," Martie said, then repeated herself louder to be heard over the rumbling. "You won't teach them a lesson! You won't hurt the right people!"

The rumbling continued, growing louder. Rocks began to separate from the tunnel wall overhead, crashing down around Martie's feet. Damn, she really was going to die in here. Some part of her—all right, a lot of her—had still expected all this to come out okay. That somehow, she'd come in, tell whatever was in here to back off, and walk out, to continue her life.

But this wasn't the worst thing, she guessed. She was dying on her own terms, on her own schedule, not when some stupid forest guardian or whatever called her, or when some jackass who selected her for the scholarship, knowing—wanting—her to die told her to. And, if nothing else, she would be with her parents, wherever one went after death. They would be waiting for her, and they would be together again.

And she wasn't going to get her soul sucked dry or whatever had happened to the other scholarship students.

Martie pried one eye open to assess the damage and how much longer she had. Her flashlight seemed to be working better in the midst of the chaos, somehow still in one piece even though she'd dropped it onto the floor. She could see it shining into the darkness inside the cavern, illuminating the crumbling rocks and the dark shape moving within.

Wait, no, that wasn't her flashlight. Martie opened both eyes. It was Alice, floating calmly through the destruction, not even flinching when debris tumbled through her. By her glow, Martie could make out the outline of the guardian, something monstrous and horned and many limbed.

"She is right," Alice said calmly, her voice somehow carrying above the ruckus of destruction. "You are destroying your hill for nothing."

The guardian's shadow calmed, and the rumbling quieted. Martie got the impression it was contemplating Alice.

You are still here. It sounded surprised. Though Martie heard the voice in her head, it was clear it was addressing Alice, who seemed very small beside the shadow and the vastness of the cavern. *Why have you not passed on, child?*

"Listen to her," Alice said again, sounding more aware, more present, than she normally did. How much energy must she be using to manifest like this? "The person you made the bargain with is dead and gone. You cannot hurt him, not on this side of the world."

What would you have me do? The shadow sagged in Alice's glow. *This is my hill, my forest. I am to guard it. I have failed. What can I do to make it right?*

Martie gingerly detached herself from the wall, stepping back to the entrance of the cavern. She hesitated for a moment at the edge of the water, then plowed ahead. Luckily, it was only ankle depth. None of the features of the forest guardian solidified in the darkness as Martie approached, except for a pair of large, glowing eyes.

"Change the bargain," Martie said.

To what? With whom? The eyes blinked. *They have defaced my hallowed hill. There must be consequences. There must be a fair trade.*

Martie looked to Alice, but the ghost merely watched her. Martie could see her eyes now, not the black depression that was normally there. She looked more real, more alive, than Martie had ever seen her. But she said nothing, offering no help.

All right, so it was up to her. Martie crossed her arms over her chest, staring down at the water circling her ankles and seeping through her boots into her socks. On one hand, there was the forest guardian, who had been protecting this section of forest and who had this hill as its home, no doubt for thousands and thousands of years, at least, since the indigenous people in the area knew of it. Probably far longer than that. Someone had come in, destroyed the forest on top of the hill, and then built the original building.

On the other hand, there was the school, small and prestigious, mostly filled with basically good—if a little naïve—kids. And a few bad apples who thought it was okay to lure people to their deaths. But mostly good, with a relatively long history.

Could they move the school? Maybe. It would lose the historical buildings and the history, though, and there would probably be pushback, though no doubt the families who attended had the funds to build elsewhere. But where? Would the forest floor be acceptable? Who "owned" the land, from a government standpoint?

That might be too much logistics to worry about.

Okay, so if the school stayed where it was, what would it take to make the forest guardian feel respected? For it to accept the school as part of its forest?

"What if the school accepted that this was your forest?" Martie mused out loud. "We could, oh, I don't know, build a statue or something. A monument. Teach about you in our classes. Lead hikes through the woods to commune with you." Like a mascot, though Martie was not going to say that out loud. That would be the best way to sell it to the school and, with a school like this, where people wanted to be, for the most part, it would be well-regarded by the students.

You would worship me? Accept me as your protector?

"Yes," Martie said with more conviction than she felt. She'd have to get other people on board. Sinclair would be down, probably, and she had the right connections. "And if I cannot hold up my part of the bargain, well, I guess you can eat my soul or whatever."

No, there would be no point. A loud sigh. *But perhaps I will destroy the buildings.*

"So, you accept?"

I will make this bargain with you. What is your name, child?

"Martie. Martina Torsney."

Martie Martina Torsney, I make this bargain with you. You and your people will show me allegiance, and I shall protect you. Do you accept?

Martie nodded as solemnly as she could manage. "Yes, I accept. What shall we call you?"

The voice said something that Martie could not hope to remember or pronounce.

"I'm afraid our limited human mouths cannot pronounce so magnificent a name." God, she was laying it on thick. "Can we call you…" She dug through her limited memory of what it'd said in her mind, searching for something pronounceable. "…Gal?"

There was a long silence. *Fine*, it finally said. *The bargain is sealed. I look forward to seeing your terms completed, Martie Martina Torsney.*

Martie bowed, since that seemed appropriate, and turned, making her way back toward the tunnel, illuminated by the faint light of her flashlight on the ground. Alice floated along just behind her, illuminating the water and the debris. Behind them, the movement of the guardian faded away. Maybe it had moved farther into the cavern. Or maybe it had gone back to sleep.

"Thank you," Alice said as they reached the tunnel.

"No, thank you." Martie scooped the flashlight back up and turned to face the ghost.

Alice shook her head. "I've been trying, for so long, to get the sacrifices to leave before they met my same fate. I have failed, every single time." She sighed, her glow starting to fade. "I never considered this course of action. That things could be changed just through talking." She smiled faintly. "You have not only saved yourself today, Martie, but every one who would have come after you. Thank you." Her glow continued to fade. Now she was just barely visible against the darkness of the cavern.

Martie's heart lurched. "Are you…are you going?"

"Yes." Her voice was barely audible. "I am finally free to pass on. Thank you, Martie."

And she was gone. Her glow, her voice, even the way the air changed when she was around. Martie reached out a hand to where Alice had been, oddly bereft at her absence. Wiping at her eyes, Martie began the trek out of the cave.

Chapter Sixteen

MARTIE HAD HARDLY made it out of the cave before Sinclair was there, hugging Martie tight.

"You're alive!" Sinclair took a step back, holding Martie at arm's length. "I can't believe it."

"Have you been waiting this whole time?" It was starting to get darker, marking it as late afternoon. "How are you not dead?" Sinclair still had mud all up her lower legs, and she had to have been out here for several hours.

Sinclair tossed her head. "I'm from Minnesota. This is nothing."

Martie's ankles, however, in their wet socks, were well on their way to freezing solid. "Well, I'm cold, and I'm exhausted. Let's get back to the dorm, and I'll tell you everything."

Something crashed behind them. Martie and Sinclair both turned to find Mr. Brooks standing there on the path, mouth agape. "What are you doing?" he exclaimed.

Oh, damn, they weren't supposed to be in the woods without a teacher. "I can explain," Martie said, cycling through possible excuses in her head and coming up with nothing that made any sense in context. "We, uh, needed some…mushrooms?" Did mushrooms even grow in caves? "Yes, for—"

"There is a *timing* for these things," Mr. Brooks continued angrily. "You are to wait until I come and get you, and then you come here. You're going to screw everything up." He clutched his head in his hands. "God, my first time, and everything is already falling apart."

He continued to mumble, but the words turned to gibberish. Martie stared at him, realization growing painfully. Mr. Brooks was the asshole. The asshole that had selected her to die, who had selected her for the scholarship knowing she was to be fed to the forest guardian. He'd been the one who'd trashed her room, who'd carved her name into the walls and table, who'd graffitied all over her locker. That's why the handwriting on the carvings had seemed familiar! And he'd had the gall to make those pictures and claim she'd drawn them, had even shown them to her and acted all concerned!

Hardly aware of what she was doing, Martie marched over to him and punched him in the face.

All that martial arts training paid off. Mr. Brooks flew backward and fell on his ass.

"You're too late," Martie said, practically vibrating. She balled her hands into fists, fingernails digging into her palms. "I've already ruined everything."

"What?" Mr. Brooks went pale as he clutched his face. "What have you done? Have you made someone else the sacrifice? Oh no. One of the real students? Oh, God."

Real students? Martie stared down at him. He was as bad as the asshat who'd made the initial bargain. He didn't see her as the same as the other students, just something to be thrown away.

"You're disgusting," Martie spat. "How could you ever think it was okay to trade a human life for something like this? For anything? You should be ashamed of yourself."

Blood trickled out of his nose, but he didn't seem to notice. "This is a very important role, one that keeps our school safe and prosperous, and I take my duties very seriously, like my predecessors before me. You understand," he said to Sinclair.

"You're a monster," Sinclair said.

Mr. Brooks ignored her. "It doesn't matter. Have your rebellion. It'll be your time soon enough."

"No, it won't." Martie crossed her arms over her chest. "And you no longer have any duties."

Mr. Brooks opened his mouth, closed it again. Finally, he seemed to rally. "Yes, you'll—"

"I changed the bargain. And the bargain is now with me, and not with you." Martie turned to Sinclair. "Seriously, let's get back to the school. I can't believe you haven't frozen to death. And that you waited. What if I hadn't come back out?"

Sinclair's eyes darted to Mr. Brooks for a second. "I mean, I would have gone back eventually." She came up next to Martie, paused for a moment, and then stepped back out onto the path, staying far away from Mr. Brooks. "Though I might have come back tomorrow. Just to see."

Martie started to follow her, then realized she was still holding the flashlight in her free hand. She clicked it off and set it down next to the mouth of the cave for someone else to use in the future, in case they needed it.

Mr. Brooks was still on the ground, spluttering. Martie ignored him, going to join Sinclair. When she looked back, the cave entrance had been replaced by the boulder again.

"How dare you?" Mr. Brooks stumbled to his feet. "How dare you just come in here, and think you can change how things are run? You are nothing. You are worth nothing. I'll...I'll change the bargain back." He stopped, staring at the boulder, then shook his head. "You'll see. You have no power here."

"No, Mr. Brooks," Martie said. "You'll see. I'm going to be the first scholarship student to graduate from Greyson. And I'm going to go on to great things."

"Miss Torsney." Near the path back to school, Mrs. Weissman leaned against a boulder, smoking a cigarette. "What are the new terms of the bargain?"

Martie blinked at her. Mrs. Weissman was in on this too? She had misjudged how many people were actually involved.

Mrs. Weissman must have noticed her look. She gave a short laugh. "No, I have never had a hand in the previous bargain. But I have been here for a long time, and I have seen the patterns. And I am familiar with the stories." Oh, yes, she'd mentioned something about local stories when introducing their mythology unit. "And Mr. Brooks has not been subtle in his actions."

Mr. Brooks glowered at her, wild and unkempt, and looking nothing like the kindly teacher persona he'd always put forward. Maybe he actually was that teacher, for the kids he deemed worth it, or maybe he only did it so he could call in favors in the future.

Mrs. Weissman took a long drag of her cigarette. "I imagine there shall be no more feeding of children to the guardian."

Martie recounted her conversation with the guardian, leaving out Alice. She'd tell Sinclair about her later. Even Mr. Brooks quieted down enough to listen to her.

"Ah, yes," Mrs. Weissman said, at one point, "the rumbling. I figured that was my cue to come and see what was happening. Oh, don't worry," she added, noting Martie's worried glance. "The school is old and well built. I suspect the damage is minor."

"A mascot?" Sinclair said when Martie had finished. She tapped one finger against her cheek. "Yes, definitely. A wonderful idea. And we can spin it as being much more prestigious than the other schools' mascots. A forest guardian, reflecting our connection with our environment and also culture and local folklore."

"Perhaps we can also update our coat of arms," Mrs. Weissman said. She dropped her cigarette, stamping it out before picking it back up and putting it in her pocket. "A tree, perhaps, or some other image that represents a forest."

"Many cultures use a white stag as a protective spirit," Sinclair replied eagerly.

"A contest, perhaps," Mrs. Weissman said. She started back up the path toward the school, lumbering slowly. "We will want an image that is evocative yet respectful. I do not suppose you can describe our particular guardian, Miss Torsney?"

Martie thought again of the shadow, huge and hulking and horned. "Not in a way that would be accurate or appealing to a general population." Hopefully that would be okay. Hopefully it would understand the spirit of the image, even if accuracy was not there.

Behind them, Mr. Brooks stood silently. Martie glanced over her shoulder discreetly. His shoulders hung, and his face was pale. He looked like a man who had lost his purpose.

Well, good.

THE LAST DAY of school was bright, sunny, and warm. Martie rolled up the sleeves of her cardigan as soon as she broke through the front doors of the school. She stood for a moment, letting the sun shine on her face. It wasn't the same as doing it back in Arizona. It didn't feel like the heat was going to peel her skin off.

Though Aunt Jessica would be here to get her soon enough, and then it was only a matter of time before the Arizona sun tried to eat her all summer.

"Okay, you." Sinclair poked her in the shoulder. "Come on, we're going to be late."

"Right."

Martie and Sinclair followed the general flow of the student body. In the middle of the lawn, between the main school building and the graveyard, a large, sheet-covered statue waited. Today, they'd unveil their new school mascot. It'd been sold as Gal the Guardian, and acceptance through the school had been quick and decisive. Martie suspected Mrs. Weissman had been the main driver behind that, but the rest of the staff had caught on pretty quickly.

Martie felt her glance drifting toward the graveyard, where Alice and the rest of the scholarship students lay. She was playing with the idea of some sort of memorial to the scholarship students. Oh, she doubted she could come out and say, *oh, yeah, all those people who have disappeared? They died and are buried here.* But maybe a plaque, noting the names and years of those who had vanished, with a note that wished that they had found peace. She needed to bounce the idea off of Sinclair. Hayden had calmed down as everything else had, but she still went pale if Martie said anything related to ghosts, or disappearances, or anything related. Maybe someday they'd be able to talk about what had happened here.

Something to worry about in the future. Now that she had a future. And she did—her scholarship was guaranteed through her graduation. Sinclair was working with her father—and through her father, the rest of the board—to expand the scholarship program. Without the sacrifice requirement in place, there was no reason why there couldn't always be at least one scholarship student, or maybe even one every year. Or maybe even a few. As Sinclair said, it wasn't like the school was hurting for money.

The students and staff gathered around the statue. Martie hadn't seen it yet—it'd been carved by some famous artist off-site and transported here overnight, so no one had. Rumor had it that it'd been carved out of wood, to symbolize the school's connection to the surrounding forest, and then sealed with something that would keep it from succumbing to the elements too quickly. Ms. Molina stood near the base. As Martie and Sinclair arrived, joining Hayden, who gave them a huge smile, Ms. Molina held up her hands, and the crowd fell silent.

"My dear friends," Ms. Molina said, her voice confident and carrying, "it is my great honor today to present to you the statue of our new school mascot. It may have taken us over a century to obtain one, but I would argue—and I'm sure you would agree—that it has been worth the wait."

Out of the corner of her eye, Martie caught Mr. Brooks hovering near the rear of the teachers. He'd not been the same since that day in the woods, and rumor had it that he would be leaving the school at the end of the year.

Good riddance.

Martie still didn't know how exactly the whole thing had worked—though it sounded like one person had been in charge of keeping up the bargain with the guardian, and the rest of it happened through procedures set up in the school's bylaws—but even knowing that she was now safe, it had been hard to keep going to chemistry and looking at him every day, knowing he had selected her to die and thought of her as less than the other students because of her background.

"Without further ado," Ms. Molina continued, "I present to you Gal the Guardian, our personal guardian of Greyson Academy." She grabbed a specific spot and pulled, and the sheet parted in the middle.

Underneath, carved in twisting wood, was the guardian. Not a proximity, not a deer like Sinclair had suggested, but like someone had reached into Martie's memory and pulled out what she'd seen in the cave that day. There were very few specifics, but the entire piece gave the elegant impression of trees and horns and branches, and a creature made out of all of them.

Martie put her hands over her mouth. It was perfect.

"Isn't it beautiful?" Ms. Molina was saying. "The artist said the image came to him in a dream. Truly an impressive piece worthy of our school."

Beside her, Sinclair reached over and wrapped one arm around hers. "You did good, Martie," she whispered.

Martie's attention drifted back to the graveyard. She had done good. And no one else would ever suffer, not like her predecessors had. She offered a silent thank you to Alice, wherever the other girl had gone. Hopefully it was somewhere beautiful, where she could be with the ones she loved. Where, perhaps, someday, Martie would join her, and Martie's parents, and everyone she, too, had loved.

But that day wouldn't be for some time.

"Come on," she said to Sinclair. "We have our whole lives in front of us."

The End

About the Author

It is a little-known fact that Kit was raised in the wild by a marauding gang of octopuses. It wasn't until she was 25 that she was discovered by a traveling National Geographic scientist and brought back to civilization. This is sometimes apparent in the way that she attempts to escape through tubes when startled.

Her transition to normalcy has been slow, but scientists predict that she will have mastered basics such as fork use sometime in the next year. More complex skills, such as proper grocery store etiquette, may be forever out of her reach.

Kit can be found cavorting about the web at her website (http://kitcampbellbooks.com).

Other books by Kit Campbell include:

Hidden Worlds

Margery Phillips finds a magic door and then manages to screw everything up. Fantasy adventure.

Shards

Eva Martinez just wants to figure out what to do with her life. Instead she gets embroiled in a millennia-old conflict. Mythic urban fantasy romance.

City of Hope and Ruin

Theo's City is infested with monsters, with nowhere to run. Briony's home is threatened by the mutilated Scarred from the North. Their only salvation may be each other. High fantasy with romance.

The Short of It

Five bite-sized stories of science fiction, fantasy, and horror.

Half-Formed Places

Four-bite-sized stories of science fiction, fantasy, and horror.

43423682R00150